Violation

This book is charged with the following offenses:

☐ Puts criminal lawyers in a bad light Code sec. 1.1

☐ Sides with victims Code sec. 9.33

☐ Uses big words Code sec. 11.99

☐ Tells the truth about criminal justice Code sec. 1.1

☐ Unsympathetic to murderers Code sec. 5.89

☐ Makes it look as if justice is for sale Code sec. 2.03

☐ Needs editing Code sec. 12.7

☐ Disparages television Code sec. 3.63

Prosecutors Will Be Violated

Prosecutors Will Be Violated

*No Matter What Crime You Committed,
It's Not Your Fault*

by Archibald Spencer

TRIGANCE PRESS

Manufactured in the United States of America

10 9 8 7 6 5 4 3 2 1

Publisher's Cataloguing-in-Publication
(Provided by Quality Books, Inc.)

   Spencer, Archibald.
        Prosecutors will be violated : no matter
        what crime you committed, it's not your fault /
        Archibald Spencer. — 1st ed.
        p. cm.
        LCCN: 98-96908
        ISBN: 0-9666271-6-4

        1. Lawyers—California—Oakland—Fiction.
        2. Criminal justice, Administration of—United
        States—Fiction. I.Title.

    PS3569.P4457P76 1999   813'54
                         QB198-1695

Cover Design and Production by Maclean & Tuminelly

Published by Trigance Press, Minneapolis
http://www.trigance.com

Dedicated to
Chris

and thanks to
Scott Edelstein
Allen Fahden
Rodney Whittaker

and
"The Weavers"

Bart Baker
Abby Davis
Linda Donaldson
Lorie Holmgren
Jerry Peterson
Peg Wangensteen

These different processes for ascertaining facts are really so many games, each with their own rules; and the facts are, as the result of the game decides.

W.S. Holdsworth, *A History of English Law*

Author's Note

This is a work of fiction. Any references which appear to have been made to present or departed persons, or to places, institutions, concepts, schools of thought, or social trends have the sole purpose of enriching the story line and are not intended to be taken literally.

For example, the Matt Tyler who appears in Chapter One is not an allusion to the Wat Tyler who led a rising against Richard II in 1381, nor does the reference to Phil Guderian, the San Francisco police chief in Chapter Seven, connote Heinz Guderian, the famed Panzer general.

DEDICATION

Ever since Ashley Blackwood won his first "not guilty" verdict, his enemies in the media and the legal profession have denounced his innovations in the practice of criminal law with the self-assured righteousness of Cardinal Torquemada watching heretics roast over slow fires. Even his untimely and sensational death failed to still their invective:

San Francisco Examiner, October 21, 1994:
Blackwood's jury speeches breached the limits of ethics, if not the law. By persuading jurors to decide cases solely on passion and prejudice, he mocked the principle that people are responsible for their acts.

Time, October 22, 1994:
Through his use of squads of expert witnesses, Blackwood turned two-day trials into three-month marathons. Jurors reached verdicts based on their desire to return to their homes and jobs, rather than on the weight of the evidence.

Not once have Ashley's colleagues in the Bar congratulated him for having snatched from death row such victims of society as Wolfgang Kreuziger, Peter Vesalius, and Tanya Dzerzhinsky, to name a few. Not once do they credit him for succoring society's rejects; tears for the downtrodden never wet their cheeks. Their only concerns are to protect their sinecures on the bench, to claw their way to senior partnerships in multi-state law firms, or to fatten their public pensions. Given the power, these lords of the law would strip away from the poor and friendless the protections of judge and jury and abandon them to the mercies of the police.

Their malice prevents them from acknowledging the brilliance of Ashley's courtroom triumphs, any one of which would have made the career of a lesser man. Who but Ashley could have obtained the reversal of Ramona Krafft's conviction of aggravated assault, when her mutilation of her husband's genitals was recorded on videotape? And who but Ashley could have led a jury to sympathize with Marty Vickers, who machine-gunned thirty-nine innocent men, women, and children? Lawyers who considered Matt Tyler's defense a hopeless task muttered about "runaway juries and incompetent judges" when Ashley secured his acquittal. Within hours after any one of his stunning "not guilty" verdicts, prosecutors who couldn't convict a serial killer of simple assault, issued press releases calling for the abolition of the jury system.

I rise above the snarls of envy to present to the impartial reader the first labor of my retirement years: the true story of Ashley Blackwood's life and his most famous trials. Without exaggeration I can say that I, who was associated with Ashley for fourteen years, am the only one in the possession of all the facts. I was his closest friend and his most highly compensated associate. But for Ashley Blackwood, I would never have been able to retire before the age of forty and devote myself to the study and practice of *belles lettres.*

It has been said that behind every successful writer there stand two people: his muse and his spouse. Without the assistance of my wife Mamie, I could never have completed this undertaking. She read through both drafts of my manuscript and her commonsense comments thinned the admittedly luxurious growth of the text. Yet —not to put too fine a point upon it— I do not hold with those who believe that literary prose is a desert which can support only the strongest nouns and verbs. I am content with the language I learned as a child of the Iron Range, as refined by years of college and law at the University of Minnesota. A graceful turn of phrase, a touch of humor, are the companions of all good writing.

I dedicate this biography to the memory of a great man in the assurance that the light of truth will always dispel the night of calumny.

Knute Rockne Olsen
Eveleth, Minnesota
Spring, 1998

ONE

On Friday, June 20, 1980, the same day Ashley Blackwood hired me as an associate, Congressman George Waller was assassinated at the Springgreen Shopping Center in Oakland. The assassin was an eighteen-year-old youth by the name of Matt Tyler. At seven in the morning on the day after the assassination, Ashley called me to come to the office and discuss the newspaper and television accounts of the crime.

When I started to work for him, Ashley was a tall and attractive man with an erect and dignified posture. His eyes were light blue and his wavy hair was combed straight back. His tailored suits fit to perfection, and his secretary made sure they were well pressed. I was his opposite: crew-cut, short, and muscular, a build that served me well in many spirited hockey matches on Minnesota's Iron Range. After an hour's review of the media reports, he said, "Knute, that Tyler kid will be my first murder defendant. He'll make my reputation." (Ashley, like me, had moved from Minnesota to California and knew that my name was pronounced "Kah-noot," not "Newt.")

Congressman Waller had been speaking to a group of

about fifty people at the grand opening of the shopping center. It was a warm day; gauzy altostratus clouds filtered the sunlight. Water from a shower the night before glistened in small puddles on the streets and parking lots. Congressman Waller spoke from a six-foot-high stage in front of the orange school bus he characterized as his "traveling campaign headquarters." The flags of the United States and California snapped in the breeze on each side of him. On the stage with Waller were Dick Whittington, the mayor of Purgatory Creek; Bill Pitt and Chuck Fox, members of the California legislature; Bob Walpole, his campaign manager; and Ben Tarleton, sheriff of Oakland County.

Representative Waller was seeking re-election for a seventh term. The subject of his talk was automobile insurance, which, along with property taxes, dominated California political discussions. Although a champion of private enterprise, Waller asserted on the one hand that the premiums charged by California auto insurers were too high, while also arguing on the other hand, that, if the state set premiums at a level which made the business unprofitable, the insurers would leave the state. He concluded by proposing that the Governor appoint an independent committee to make recommendations to the legislature.

Matt stood near the front of the crowd. The media accounts described him as five feet, eight inches in height, thin, long-haired, with a pale, washed-out appearance, as if he had been bleached once too often. He wore black slacks cut off at the ankles, white cotton socks, worn leather sandals, a faded red T-shirt, and a black nylon jacket. For two days he had followed Waller's campaign bus in a battered, yellow Fiat convertible. When Waller's bus stopped, Matt stopped, and whenever Waller addressed the public, Matt worked his way towards the front of the audience. Matt was adamant that the state should limit automobile insurance premiums to fifty dollars a year.

As Congressman Waller made his concluding remarks, Matt reached into a holster underneath his shoulder, pulled out a Colt .32 caliber automatic, and fired three shots. The first two shots hit Waller, one in the chest and one in the shoulder. The third shot missed and lodged in the podium. The chest wound was instantly fatal. Waller fell dead beneath the California flag.

Matt was about to fire again when Franz Held, a burly rancher, threw him to the ground and hog-tied him with his belt. Only then did Sheriff Tarleton rush to Held's side to read him his rights and call for assistance. Four squad cars arrived in minutes and took Matt to jail. As he was led away, two spectators heard him say, "There are more bullets where those came from."

Within the hour, reporters and photographers from the San Francisco *Chronicle* and *Examiner*, a dozen regional publications, and four television channels, pulsed like maggots around the modest frame house of Hedley and Elmira Tyler, Matt's parents. When a *Chronicle* reporter told them that their only child was an assassin, all they could say was, "I don't believe it. He's a good boy. He wouldn't hurt a fly."

From the Tyler's house the media rampaged across San Mateo, Contra Costa, and Alameda counties. They shoved microphones into the faces of Matt's relatives, teachers, acquaintances, and classmates; dug through police records, motor vehicle reports, and school report cards; and interviewed anyone who had any connection, no matter how tenuous, to Matt or his parents. The consensus in the media was that Matt was a loner who never had a date or a friend, was a mute in class, performed at a low level, and never participated in athletics. The police learned that he possessed a .44 caliber Ruger and a .38 caliber Beretta in addition to his .32 caliber Colt, and practiced marksmanship two or three times a week.

Having decided to take on the case, Ashley's major concern was how to induce Matt or the court to appoint him as counsel, when he had had no experience trying homicide cases. Fortunately, the name of Matt's father, Hedley Tyler, rang a chime in Ashley's memory. He checked his client index and found that he had defended Hedley on a drunk driving charge a year ago when he crashed into a utility pole at 2 A.M. The police found him unconscious and reeking of alcohol; a breathalyzer test showed he had a .15 alcohol level, well over the permissible limit.

Hedley's was not a promising case, even for one of Ashley's talents, but, as it happened, the prosecutor was leaving for a month's vacation in Europe and wanted to clear his desk before departure. Ashley worked out a package deal to settle Hedley's case and a dozen other pending DUI files for pleas of reckless driving. Hedley was over-joyed with the result; it was his second offense and a conviction would have resulted in an extended jail sentence. He promised to call Ashley if he had any more legal problems.

Without waiting for Hedley to remember his vow, Ashley appeared at the Tyler house just as Hedley was attempting to open his door to escape the reporters and lawyers who had circled his house like a war party of Mohawks around a pioneer stockade. Ashley had a police medallion given him by a friend on the San Francisco force. By holding it in front of him and shouting "police, police," he made his way through the crowd to Hedley's side. Hedley recognized him and let him into the house.

Ashley told Hedley that Matt needed the best possible legal representation and that he would be glad to provide it for whatever fee Hedley and Elmira could afford. They signed a contract Ashley had brought with him which stip-ulated that Ashley would handle the trial for $30,000 and that Hedley and Elmira would render all the assistance Ashley requested, including Matt's signature to the contract. The agreement also provided that Ashley would receive 50 percent of all book, movie, and television rights emanating from the assassination and the trial. Ashley suspected that the Tylers could afford a fee double the amount required by the contract, but he assured me he wasn't in the case for money. Years later he was delighted to learn that his agent had sold the story rights for several times the amount of his retainer from the Tylers. It eventually became a movie entitled *The Lonely Assassin*. The crime, however, never became the subject of a television docudrama, as it would nowadays when the murder is reenacted on the air before the victim's blood has dried.

Since Matt was Ashley's first murder defendant, the media assumed that Ashley would enter a plea of insanity. When Matt pleaded not guilty at the arraignment, courthouse reporters predicted that the prosecution would eat Ashley alive. They neglected, however, to take into account the brilliance Ashley had displayed in his previous criminal trials.

After graduating from the Stanford School of Law in 1973, Ashley joined the old-line San Francisco firm of Lynch & Jeffries. On the day of his hire, he asked the partners to assign him their criminal defense work, and they were delighted to honor his request.

He started by representing persons accused of traffic violations. In such cases, the trial judge tends to ignore any testimony contrary to the sworn statements of the arresting officer and may even issue a ruling without bothering to let the defense present its case. After two summary defeats, Ashley concluded that he could obtain acquittals only if he demolished the arresting officer's credibility on cross-examination during the state's case.

Ashley had an amazing ability to extract information

from confidential records. With a few words to a custodian, he obtained access to files others could reach only through court orders. "People want to be helpful, Knute," he confided to me. "You just have to find the tone that makes them vibrate to your pitch." He managed to gather complete transcripts of the testifying officer's high school, academy, and personnel records. At trial he offered in evidence everything he had discovered which reflected adversely on the officer's character, such as drunkenness on duty, suspicion of withholding confiscated narcotics, engaging in adulterous liaisons, shoplifting, income tax fraud, or unsportsman-like conduct.

When the prosecution bayed objections to the introduction of this evidence as irrelevant and immaterial, Ashley responded, "Your Honor, officer Schweik is the state's sole witness. The prosecution's entire case hangs on his testimony. Since officer Schweik is an agent of the state of California, it is presumed that he is telling the truth. He speaks, as it were, robed in the sanctity of office. But Your Honor well knows it is a fundamental principle of our common law that each side is entitled to challenge the testimony of a witness for the other side. When I present a witness for the defense, I expect the state to utilize every means at its disposal to tarnish his or her reputation for probity and veracity. The defense has an equal right to test the prosecution's witnesses."

Because of the precedents set by the California Court of Appeals, the trial judge had to admit Ashley's proffer of character evidence. Prosecuting attorneys found that what

7

was supposed to be a half-hour traffic matter became an all-day state trial. More to the point, once officers discovered that Ashley represented the defendant, no threat by the prosecution had the power to force them to take the witness stand. As a result, the prosecution had to settle for a greatly reduced charge or dismiss the case.

From this experience Ashley derived his first black-letter Rule: *STOP AT NOTHING TO DEMOLISH HOSTILE WIT-NESSES*. This Rule, along with his other Rules, he had engraved on brass plaques and, when he had his own firm and his own building, mounted them on the walls of the John Marshall Conference Room.

The partners of Lynch & Jeffries were delighted with Ashley's work and advanced him to the defense of rape cases. Here Ashley's technique of demolishing the character of a witness proved of enormous value, and he confided in me that he never felt challenged by rape cases. "In traffic cases," he said, "all that checking on an officer's background was terribly time-consuming and expensive. In a rape case, the old boyfriends flocked to me like chickadees to a feeder. They couldn't wait to tell me all they knew about the victim's sex life and addictions."

The first hour of Ashley's cross-examination of the alleged victim invariably reduced her to a state where she was unable to continue her testimony, and the state had to withdraw all charges. Prosecutors, judges, and law school professors railed that Ashley's withering cross-examinations and parades of witnesses were irrelevant to the issue whether, in a specific instance, the complainant had overtly or impliedly consented to sexual intercourse. Ashley's motivation, they asserted, was not to elicit the facts, but to intimidate the complainant into dropping her charges. And it is undeniable that many alleged victims, on learning that Ashley had been retained to represent the defendant, refused to proceed or found themselves "unable" to identify the defendant or left town.

Ashley never responded to these or any other accusations. One of his black letter Rules was: *NEVER SAY ANYTHING UNLESS IT ADDS TO YOUR CASE.* He never submitted to oral interviews, since he well knew the predilection of reporters and editors to engage in deliberate misquotation so as to make a "story." He taped all his telephone conversations and had his secretary transcribe them. He never spoke to clients except in his office, which he swept for "bugs" every morning. If he had to interview a client in jail, he demanded a "safe" room and utilized a voice scrambler.

After five years with Lynch & Jeffries, Ashley had become California's leading specialist in the defense of civil and criminal rape cases. He received lucrative referrals from all over the state, but mostly from lawyers in Los Angeles, where there had been an eruption of rape charges against men of prominence in the screen world.

His fame and the magnitude of his retainers entitled him, he thought, to partnership status, but the partners of Lynch & Jeffries informed him that they never advanced an associate until he or she had completed a full eight years of practice with the firm. They refused to waive the rule in Ashley's case, so on July 10, 1978, Ashley resigned from Lynch & Jeffries and founded Blackwood & Associates.

In Matt's case, Ashley did not attempt to formulate a defense strategy until he had spent weeks talking to Matt, his parents, and his classmates. As a matter of form, he peppered the court with motions to suppress certain types of evidence, including Matt's statement that there were "more bullets where those came from." To confuse the prosecution, he made other motions indicating that his client would plead insanity as a defense. Ashley trusted me, a lawyer a few months out of Minnesota Law School, to prepare all the motion papers and even argue some. When I reported that the court had denied a motion, Ashley smiled and said, "Never mind, Knute; it doesn't matter. We're just trying to keep the prosecution busy. If a few motions stick, that's fine. It's a good show, and it makes the client think we're working hard. Plus it gets my name in the paper."

At the arraignment Ashley made Matt dress in a dark suit and tie. Elmira and Hedley dogged our steps with tear-swollen eyes. She always wore a neat housedress; he, clean chino slacks and a sweater. At all the proceedings, we could count on them to provide an ostinato of muted sobs.

The various motions produced only one controversy of interest to the media. Ashley demanded that our experts be allowed to examine the shell casings recovered from the scene of the crime. The prosecution produced four, all the same caliber as Matt's pistol. Ashley moved that the prosecution be barred from offering any of them at the trial on the grounds that the unanimous testimony of the eyewitnesses was that only three shots had been fired. He implied that the fourth shell casing was a "plant" to create the impression that Matt was a frustrated mass murderer, bent on killing all within pistol range.

"This, Your Honor," he said, "is typical of the way the prosecution has handled this case from first to last. Rather than letting the world see that Matt is a confused and troubled child, the prosecution has conspired to portray him as an executioner in the mold of a Stalin by littering the ground with shell casings. Since when has it been the office of the prosecutor to create a crime scenario, rather than portray it as it is? Do the attorneys for the state have a charter to characterize confused children, such as defendant, as homicidal maniacs? We admit that defendant held a pistol in his hand on June 20, but we will show that it was his only offense." With this "teaser," Ashley sat down.

The prosecutor, Arabella Warren, countered by arguing that the defendant's motion required the state to produce *all* shell casings recovered at the scene of the crime and that the police had complied with the motion. Which of the casings came from Matt's pistol, she said, would be a matter for testimony at the trial.

The motion to exclude the shell casings was denied. To my surprise, Ashley was far from disappointed.

"Knute," he said, "I expected it to be denied. The point is, we got our story in two papers and on three TV channels. Not bad, I'd say. And we planted the seed of our defense."

I had no idea what Ashley's defense would be, so I said nothing and waited until Ashley saw fit to reveal his master plan.

People v. Tyler came to trial on October 20, 1980. Ashley and I had been working on it for four months to the exclusion of all other business. Ashley told me that, even taking into account the Tyler's $30,000 retainer, Blackwood & Associates' receipts averaged $14,000 less per month than they had for the same months the previous year. Only the firm's solid core of negligence cases and the accumulated fees from two years of rape cases, allowed it to meet the weekly payroll. It is a tribute to Ashley's management that Blackwood & Associates never had to delay or cut the salaries of its staff and associates.

Ashley was fluent in the rules of evidence and criminal procedure and seldom labored over legal technicalities. During his five years with Lynch & Jeffries, he had compiled forms of motion papers and legal briefs on hundreds of points of criminal law and procedure and stored them on floppy disks, so that, when we prepared motion papers, we simply filled in a few blanks and served the documents. At that time the legal profession had yet to appreciate the computer's ability to inundate the opposition in a sea of paper. Arabella Warren, Matt's prosecutor, complained that Ashley's incessant demands for documents forced her to divert her staff to shepherding paperwork instead of preparing for trial.

Our talks with Matt confirmed the dismal strain of the media reports: he was friendless, a poor student, a loner—in short, what his classmates called a "zero." He attended school with commendable regularity, but was a low C student even in the days of grade inflation. He showed no talent in any academic discipline and participated in no extra-curricular activities.

We learned that a classmate had stolen Matt's pistols from a sporting-goods store and sold them to Matt at bargain prices. We also found out that Matt was a chronic liar, forcing us to check every fact he volunteered. For instance, he said he had bought his derelict Fiat convertible from his earnings, but couldn't tell us how he earned the money. We knew that it was a gift from his parents, as reported in the press.

I was dispirited by the progress of our research. "Frankly," I said to Ashley, "we don't have a thing to work with. Except for buying guns a year ago, there's no pattern of hostility, no outbursts against his parents or friends or teachers. The guy's a nothing, a blank page. What's our defense going to be?"

Ashley jerked his head up from the transcript he was reading. "What did you just say?"

"I said he was a blank and—"

He waved me to silence and eased back in his chair, closed his eyes, and for the first time in my experience went into one of his "trances," a period of intense mental activity when his mind was cut off from the sensations of the outside world. It lasted ten minutes. When he opened his eyes, he looked at me and said, "*Tabula rasa!*

You're right, Knute. That's exactly what he is, an empty slate. That means we can write on him anything we want."

I didn't know what Ashley had in mind. The concept of an empty slate meant nothing to me in law, although I had heard of the term once in a philosophy course. I begged him to tell me more, but Ashley, like the showman he was, told me all would come clear at the trial and I should now concentrate my research on the relationship between Matt and his parents.

Neither Hedley nor Elmira Tyler were prepossessing in appearance. Hedley's manner was wispy and hesitant; he seldom finished a sentence he had begun. He had a spare frame to which a potbelly had attached itself, as if it were a module purchased separately from the rest of his body. Black-rimmed glasses circled his eyes and gave him a misty look, due partly to the thickness of the lenses and partly to the dirt accumulated on their surfaces. After receiving an honorable discharge from the Army in 1946, Hedley had attended the University of California in Berkeley under the GI bill. He majored in Organic Chemistry on the assumption that there would be a huge post-war demand for plastics. After three years, he met and married Elmira and dropped out of college. Hedley never kept a job for more than two years and never attained a position much above entry level. He seemed content with his modest means and claimed that, if his family circumstances had been different, he might have attained a position that gave full scope to his talents.

While Hedley was "laid back," Elmira frothed with discontent. She had put herself through nursing school and held jobs at two hospitals. She railed at a system which made her a slave to doctors, none of whom, in her opinion, had half her medical knowledge. Elmira had a four-square build and a loud voice, but her conversation had no focus. I never asked her one question without her answering a totally different one. I learned not to ask directly about a subject on which I needed information, and instead asked questions at random in the hope that she would wander into my area of interest.

Both of them considered Matt "a fine, upstanding boy, not the brightest, but solid." They were content if he received Cs. They respected his privacy, let him follow his interests, never entered his room without permission, and had no idea that he owned three pistols.

His classmates neither liked nor disliked him. To them he was like a tree or a rock: he was "just there."

On his eighteenth birthday Hedley and Elmira gave Matt a yellow Fiat convertible Matt had spotted in a used-car lot. Once behind the wheel, he expected his status among his classmates to sprout from invisibility to popularity. The only reaction came from one classmate who said it was "cool." Within a week, Matt was once more invisible. A few months before the assassination, Matt began practicing with his pistols at a firing range. Judging by his results on June 20, he must have become a reasonable marksman, if not a sharpshooter. He boasted at school that he was a "crack shot and they'd be hearing more about him pretty soon." A classmate repeated Matt's boast to her mother, who called Elmira and asked her whether she was aware that her son owned a pistol and claimed to be a crack shot. Elmira told her she must be confusing Matt with another classmate because Matt was a quiet, sensitive boy who hated guns and violence.

Ashley and I never determined why Matt selected Representative Waller as his target. We guessed that, since Waller had campaigned aggressively throughout the district, his frequent appearances made him a target of opportunity. Another possibility was that Matt's father had insisted that Matt pay his own automobile insurance, so that Representative Waller became Matt's scapegoat for the horrendous expense of insuring a sports car owned by an eighteen-year-old California male.

People v. Tyler was my first jury trial. I was nervous and felt unprepared, and dreaded the moment when jury selection ended, the opening statements were made, and the first witness was called. Even though I had no speaking role, I lived in fear that I would forget to remind Ashley of some important weakness in a witness's testimony or some flaw in an exhibit. Over the years I gained composure, but, as long as I practiced law, the announcement of a trial date deprived me of my appetite for the rest of the day.

Ashley, by contrast, literally rubbed his hands together in anticipation of the contest, as excited as a ten-year-old lad going to a new horror movie. A courtroom ambush, such as the recantation of his star witness or the demolition of the testimony of his most respected expert, never raised his heartbeat. He acted as if he had expected that development and was delighted that the other side had stumbled into his trap. Once outside the courthouse, however, he reacted quickly and effectively, issued directions to his staff to locate another expert, no matter the cost, and to come up with a plan to impeach his own witness. To make sure the work was done properly, he remained in the office with us through the night. No matter how late he worked, he looked fresh and crisp the next morning in the courtroom. While I and the other associates yawned, he pushed, prodded, and objected without letup.

People v. Tyler presented no surprise evidence. The state had solid eyewitnesses, and Ashley did not try to discredit them. The only questions he directed to them regarded Matt's appearance at the time Representative Waller was shot: did he appear nervous, angry, or happy? The witnesses testified that they couldn't detect any emotion on Matt's face; he appeared as calm and disinterested as if he were listening to a sermon.

The state produced the history of the Colt .32, showing when and from whom Matt bought it, and where he purchased the shells. The owner of the pistol range testified that he had seen Matt fire it many times in the months preceding the assassination. Three shell casings and three bullets were identified to Matt's Colt. The controversial fourth shell casing came from another weapon of unknown make and ownership. The jury exchanged thoughtful glances when Ashley cornered the state's ballistics expert into admitting that the shell could have been fired from the type of pistol employed by the KGB. That admission made the next day's front pages.

When the prosecution rested, Ashley put a number of Matt's relatives, classmates, and acquaintances on the stand to testify how each of them perceived Matt as a person. All except Hedley and Elmira said he was a "zero," a nullity, a blank. They couldn't imagine that he would ever resort to violence, unless it was to gain attention. When a classmate was asked whether Matt had in fact gained attention as a result of the assassination, she replied, "You damn right! He's all we talk about in class."

The testimony of the witnesses was so uniform that several times the state moved its exclusion as repetitious and irrelevant. In deference to the judge and jury, and feeling his point had been made, Ashley, struck six names from the witness list.

Matt never took the stand. During the trial, he received four well-paying invitations to appear on talk shows. Ashley insisted that he decline all of them.

I now began to see the direction of Ashley's defense and was not entirely surprised when he stood up and delivered his famous *"tabula rasa"* closing argument:

"Ladies and gentlemen of the jury, the purpose of this trial is to answer one question. The prosecution insists that the question is, 'Who shot Representative Waller?' That, we submit, is the wrong question. We concede that Matt Tyler was at the Springgreen Shopping Center on

June 20 and that he held in his hand a Colt .32 automatic and pointed it at Congressman Waller. That much we admit. But the real question is, 'Who pulled the trigger?'

"Yes, Matt bought the pistol, Matt bought the shells, Matt aimed the weapon. But Society pulled the trigger. Yes, ladies and gentlemen of the jury, Society pulled the trigger.

"Let us look back at what we have heard at this trial.

"Who was Matt Tyler? No one really knows. His parents who raised him and nurtured him—all they could say about him was that he was a 'good boy,' that he was 'average,' that he was 'quiet,' that he was 'obedient,' that he 'kept to himself.' Did they describe him as vital, interesting, charming, noisy, hell-raising, artistic, exciting, handsome, willful, mischievous? No, they said; he was 'quiet,' 'average,' 'obedient,' 'private.' A nothing.

"What did his classmates and teachers say of him? That he was a 'loner,' 'quiet,' 'inconspicuous,' 'average'—and the word that sums it all up—a 'zero.'

"Matt Tyler, a living, breathing, human being, was a 'zero,' a nothing, an empty slate, ready to receive whatever might be written on it.

"So, who wrote on the empty slate of Matt Tyler? Was it the church, the school, his parents? No, if these had written on Matt, he would not be in this courtroom today. It was Society and Society alone.

"And what did Society write on Matt's empty slate? Did it write that good is rewarded, evil punished? You and I laugh, ladies and gentlemen of the jury, we laugh. Did

Society write that if you work hard and go to college, you will be looked up to? We laugh. Nowadays adults with postgraduate degrees flip hamburgers to survive.

"So what did Society write on the mind of Matt Tyler? Newspapers, magazines, television programs, all wrote over and over on his young mind, 'Commit a crime, kidnap a child, engage in espionage, shoot the President, do any of these and you will be famous.'

"That, ladies and gentlemen of the jury, is what Society wrote. Does anyone doubt it? Pick up any newspaper, any magazine, tune to any television channel, any radio station. What do you find? Young men and women studying, preparing for college, working hard, and advancing by patient effort into the ranks of doctors, lawyers, and business leaders? No, of course not. You see murder, rape, arson, embezzlement, divorce, and wife beating. You see that the men and women who commit these crimes are talked about everywhere. The media all say, 'Pull the trigger and you will be famous.'

"So I come back to the question, 'Who pulled the trigger?' Was it Matt Tyler? No, Matt just stood there with his pistol. Matt was a tool. It was Society, our Society, that pulled the trigger."

Such was the peroration of Ashley's *"tabula rasa"* defense, the most famous jury address since Clarence Darrow's summation in the *Scopes* trial. It gave rise to one of Ashley's famous black letter Rules: *WHEN YOU CAN'T PUT IT ON SOMEBODY ELSE, PUT IT ON SOCIETY.*

While the jury retired to deliberate, I asked Ashley what verdict he expected the jury to return.

"A deadlock or an acquittal."

I thought Ashley was being optimistic, and was astonished when the jury returned in two days with a verdict of "not guilty."

Overnight Ashley became a celebrity and cases came to him from every corner of the state. But none of his trials, not even his defense of Ellen Strafford, a woman whose beauty will forever haunt my imagination, better displayed his ability to win an "impossible" case.

TWO

The following story appeared in the *San Francisco Examiner* on Saturday, August 22, 1981:

MILLIONAIRE THOMAS W. STRAFFORD KILLED IN BLAST; HOUSE LEVELED; CHAUFFEUR ALSO KILLED

A car bomb that yesterday rocked the elite Naseby Hills area of San Francisco County claimed the lives of Thomas Wentworth ("Buzz") Strafford and his chauffeur, Juan Fangio.

Ellen Strafford, the wife of the late Mr Strafford, was riding her horse behind the Strafford residence at the time of the blast. The noise of the explosion startled her horse, and it threw her to the ground, breaking her left arm.

Mr Strafford was one of the early entrepreneurs of Silicon Valley. He founded SoftState Technologies in 1972 and sold it for a reputed 200 million dollars in 1977. He followed up this success by founding MicroVision Products in 1978, and selling it two years later to IBM for 450 million dollars of IBM stock.

He married the former Ellen Pym Stuart in 1980. Mrs Strafford was the daughter of the late J.B. Pym, a well-known banker and art collector, and the grand-daughter of Mahmet Arazi, the Prime Minister of Lebanon who was assassinated in 1962 by members of the rival Rashad clan. Mrs Strafford was then a child of twelve.

Police department detective Rollie Rupert refused to give any further information as to the cause of the blast or the possible motivation of the perpetrators. Mrs Strafford was not available for comment.

Besides Mrs Strafford, the decedent was survived by two children of his first marriage, Margaret Strafford Laud of Saint Louis, Missouri, and Thomas Wentworth Strafford, Jr, of Sherman Oaks, California.

From the *San Francisco Chronicle* two days later:

At a press conference at the Holiday Inn in Naseby Hills, detective Rollie Rupert yesterday said that his office had not yet determined any motive for the murders of "Buzz" Strafford and his chauffeur last Saturday. He refused to speculate whether the two men were victims of an extortion plot. Nor would he confirm rumors that the murder was the work of an amateur, since the blast seemed more powerful than needed to kill the occupants of the vehicle.

"We are following any and all leads," detective Rupert said. "In a case like this, we spend days walking down blind alleys so as to leave no stone unturned."

I read these articles with no more than my usual detached professional interest, since it never occurred to me that Blackwood & Associates would play a leading part in this tragedy. Although my life in the law has inured me to surprise, I must admit I was taken aback when Ashley came to my office the morning of August 26 and asked me to attend a meeting with him and Ellen Strafford in our largest conference room!

As I watched her enter, I felt the presence of a beauty different from that of any other woman I had ever seen in person, print, pastel, or oil, a beauty which combined perfection of face and figure with an aura of spiritual enlightenment. Her eyes, warm as the Mediterranean air, shone with a light that could have been sent only by the Lord. Her voice rang with the melody of a distant harp. She wore a black silk dress which fit snugly over her well-proportioned form; her left arm lay in a cast supported by a yellow silk scarf fashioned into a sling.

The offices of Blackwood & Associates were then located in a brick building on Market Street and lacked the tasteful appointments which surrounded us four years later in the Blackwood Building, but Ellen's presence suffused the bare walls and oak chairs of Conference Room 2 with a luminosity never attained by the palaces of the software millionaires.

I could not imagine what business a woman of such wealth and prestige would have with Ashley and me. I held my breath until she said with a smile, "I'm afraid, gentlemen, that I'm here to solicit your assistance on a personal matter. Let me assure you that my concerns are not of a criminal nature, even though they are related to the death of my husband. I made a terrible mistake, and I know that you, and only you" — she included me in her gaze — "only you two, with your knowledge of a world unknown to me, can guide me. I am quite prepared to pay any sum you name. As a show of good faith, I have brought a $250,000 retainer."

I tried not to look at Ashley, as I'm sure he tried not to look at me. Nevertheless, our eyes met. In that instant I knew that he, no more than any other man, could not resist the appeal of this goddess.

Ashley cleared his throat, steepled his fingers, leaned back in his chair, and said, "Am I to understand, Mrs Strafford, that the police consider you a suspect in the murder of your husband?"

A look of bemused shock crossed her face. "Certainly not! That possibility has never occurred to me and, thank heaven, it has never occurred to Rollie Rupert and his Keystone Kops." She shook her head. "I shouldn't speak of Rollie this way. He means well, I know, but, really, he must have brought every officer in the county to poke around the ruins of the lovely house Buzz and I built. Everything my Edsel and Sairey had straightened and cleaned, Rollie's men turned upside down. As if we hadn't been through enough already!"

She looked down and made an effort to hold back her tears. I offered my handkerchief, but she refused it with a shake of her head that caused two tears to roll down her perfect cheeks. "No," she said, "I'm afraid Buzz and I made our biggest mistake right at the beginning when we received the first note."

Ashley leaned forward. "What note?"

"The threats." She pulled several sheets of paper from her purse. "I copied them. The police have the originals."

Ashley glanced at the papers and handed them to me.

They followed the time-honored style of ransom demands, words cut from newspaper headings and glued to a sheet of drugstore paper.

"I put them in sequence," she said. "Those are my numbers and dates in the upper right-hand corner."

The first note read, "Strafford, two million or your life. Unmarked twenties and hundreds in cardboard box in dumpster behind 2295 Marigold Road 2 AM Tuesday." The second one read, "Last chance. No more fooling. Three million. 13392 Camellia Drive behind house 3 AM Wenesday [sic]." The third and last note: "You asked for it."

"When did you receive these?" Ashley inquired.

"The first one came on Monday, the seventeenth, four days before—before the explosion on Friday. The second one was on Tuesday. The last one, Thursday, the day before."

"Did you leave the money at either place?"

"We didn't take the first note seriously. We thought it was a hoax. Then on Tuesday we received the second note. It was tied to Ferdie's leg—"

"Ferdie?"

"Ferdie, my little dachshund." She wiped her eyes. "He was lying by our front door. His throat...his throat...."

"Was cut?"

"Yes. The note was taped to his little paw." She paused and took a deep breath. "Buzz and I put the money together, and we hired Booth to—"

"Booth?"

"Booth Protection Services, the security team Buzz uses—used—at his office. We hired them to help us, but they couldn't find Camellia Drive for a long time. It turned out it was in a new subdivision and not on any map. By the time they got there with the money, it was five in the morning, two hours too late."

"Whose house was it?"

"It belonged to a developer. It hadn't been sold."

"What about the developer? What did they find out about him?"

"Not a thing, Mr Blackwood. They couldn't make any connection. The police think the address was used because the house was vacant."

"Where did you find the first and last notes?"

"The first one was taped to our front door. Buzz found it when he picked up the newspaper about 7:30. The last one was taped to the windshield of his car. It was parked outside the restaurant where we'd had dinner Thursday. The chauffeur found it."

"The same chauffeur who was killed?" I asked.

"No, it was Edsel. Juan, dear Juan, had Sunday off. Poor man! He was going to retire this year."

This time Ellen accepted my handkerchief. Ashley waited for her to compose herself before asking, "You said you came to see us because of a mistake you made. The first one was not taking the first note seriously. Was there another?"

I clenched my fingernails into my palms while waiting for her answer. What kind of mistake could she have made, this woman with the beauty and demeanor of a saint? Ashley's face was unreadable; he wore the same impassive look he assumes while waiting for the foreman to announce the jury's verdict.

Ellen must have noticed our expressions because she gave a little laugh and said, "Gentlemen, please, you look so serious. Do you think I came here to ask you to defend me?" She leaned over and patted my clenched fist with her bare hand and said, "No, what I said was that Buzz and I made a mistake. I didn't say I committed murder." I sighed at the same time she laughed. "No, the mistake was when we found the second note—"

"You called Booth instead of the police," I said.

"Yes, we made a huge mistake, and that's why I came to see you. I realize now we should have called in the police and the FBI right away."

"Booth has a good reputation, but not for this kind of case," Ashley said. "So, why didn't you call the police?"

Ellen folded her hands on her lap. "I'm afraid that's a long story. Could I have something to drink? Some mint tea, if it's not too much trouble." Ashley glanced at me and I called my secretary to bring in a tray of hot water, assorted tea bags, coffee, and the chocolate chip cookies my wife Mamie bakes every week for the office.

After taking a sip of tea, Ellen said, "The reason we didn't call the police goes back many years, back to the saddest day of my life. Do you have time to talk right now? Are you expecting someone else?" Ashley said we had all day, if necessary, and asked her to proceed. "Charles Stuart, my first husband, and I lived in Lebanon for a year."

"Lebanon?" I asked.

"Yes. I have family there—that is, I had family. They were all murdered by members of the Rashad clan in 1962. I'm half Lebanese, you see."

That, I thought, explains her exotic beauty.

"Charles was an idealist. He felt that he had a duty to do whatever he could to stop the fighting among the factions in Beirut. But he also had a practical side. He was quite poor when we were married, and he knew that idealists without funds never accomplish much. We married after he received his Ph.D. from Michigan State in 1970."

"You knew each other in college?" Ashley asked.

"He was in the graduate school of Engineering. I was an undergraduate in Fine Arts. We met at a dance. After we were married, he bought a small computer company and we moved to Minneapolis."

Ashley and I exchanged smiles. Everybody seems to live in Minneapolis at some time in their lives.

"The company was a great success. He sold it after three years and decided to dedicate himself to the study of comparative religions. He honestly believed that if people understood each other's religions, they would become more tolerant of their differences. As I said, he was very idealistic.

"We moved to Lebanon and Charles began studying comparative religions at the American University in Beirut. Then, quite suddenly, the factional fighting escalated. Two of our friends were abducted and held for ransom, and another was shot on the street for no apparent reason other than that he was a U.S. citizen. The American ambassador told us to leave before we became targets. Charles was reluctant to go, but I managed to convince him that killers and kidnappers have no interest in the religion or the *Weltanschauung* of their victims. They kill for the love of killing.

29

"We planned to leave on August 17, 1976, but two days before our departure, Charles was abducted as he left his afternoon class at the American University. That evening I received a call demanding one million dollars in ransom."

"Do you have any idea, Mrs Strafford, who abducted your husband?" Ashley asked.

"We never found out. I always felt that it was someone in the Rashad family. That's the family that massacred my grandfather and all his descendants, except me. I am the only surviving Arazi. The police thought the kidnappers were a splinter group of the True Sons of Allah. But, honestly, Mr Blackwood, who knows? They're all murderers. I couldn't handle it. I collapsed and called our good friend Nikos Callimachus. He told me to call the police."

"And you did," I said.

"I did, and I've always wished I hadn't. Nikos had good intelligence in the Lebanese Christian community. Someone tipped him off where Charles was being held and told him that Charles would never come out alive, even if we paid the ransom. Nikos said we had to send in a team at once to rescue Charles before he was killed. It was the only way, he said, and I had to rely on his knowledge of the Mideast.

"I asked him who would be the best one to conduct the operation. At that time there were any number of guns for hire. You could buy a respectable army if you had the money. I thought we should hire some Israelis. Everybody was impressed by their raid on Entebbe in July. Nikos said no, the police, the Christian police, were the best for this job. He was friendly with a captain on the force, and the captain assured him he would select his best men to carry out the rescue.

"I agonized over what to do. After debating the alternatives a hundred times, I felt I had no choice but to trust Nikos's judgment. I gave him all the cash we had in our account and all my jewelry. The police captain assembled a group of his best men to conduct a dawn raid. But somebody leaked our plan. When the police entered the house, they found Chuck dead on the floor, the house empty. I left Beirut that night and moved to a condominium in Carmel. That's where I met Buzz. His wife had died of cancer the year before. He'd sold his house and moved into the same building."

She paused. "You asked why I didn't call the police. They failed me once, and I wasn't going to let them fail me again."

After several minutes of silence Ashley said, "So you came to see us because you think the police will find it suspicious that you didn't call them in the beginning?"

"Yes. I've heard that detective Rupert has a big ego."

"Where were you when Mr Strafford was killed? The newspapers said you were out riding. Is that correct?"

"Yes, it was a nice day. I always get up early, have a light breakfast, and exercise my horse, Muffin, for two hours unless the weather's bad. The blast spooked Muffin, I fell and"—she looked down at her broken arm—"this happened."

Ashley asked where the car had been for the twenty-four hours before the explosion, who had access to it, and what other cars she and Mr Strafford owned. He also asked her if she knew the provisions of Mr Strafford's will.

"I haven't seen it since our wedding in 1980," she said.

"Do you remember what it provided?"

She smiled. "Ah, yes, motive. You should know that Buzz and I signed an antenuptial agreement which provided that one-third of his estate went to me and the rest to his children. Let me point out that the agreement also provided that one-third of my estate would go to Buzz and the rest to various charities. My personal estate, I should add, is not inconsiderable, thanks to my father and my first husband."

"Do you have children?" I asked.

"Sadly, no."

Ashley asked whether she was worried that someone might select her as his next target.

"Of course. I'm selling the house and moving to a high-security apartment. You are the only ones who will know where I am."

"The police might want to talk to you again," I said. "Did you tell them about your move?"

She shook her head. "No, they'll have to reach me through you. I don't trust them or anyone else right now except, of course, you"—my heart paused as she smiled at me—"and Mr Blackwood."

"I understand," Ashley said. "There's no reason for you to talk to the police at all, Mrs Strafford. In fact, I strongly advise against it. If they need information, they can talk to me."

We spent a few minutes discussing communications and the likely progress of the case. As she left, she placed on the conference table a $250,000 cashier's check. Ashley's eyes widened slightly, but he let it lie. He disliked touching money.

Ashley escorted her to the door, and by a nod of his head indicated that I should stay in the room. When he returned, I said, "That's got to be the easiest money we've ever made."

Ashley dropped into his chair. "I don't think so, Knute. I think there's a lot more to the story than she told us— like the death of her first husband."

I stood up and almost shouted, "Surely you can't suspect this gorgeous woman of plotting her husband's death. You're joking, aren't you?"

"No, Knute, I'm not. For Heaven's sake, sit down! I get very suspicious when two rich husbands are murdered within five years."

I searched Ashley's face for the hint of a smile, but he was dead serious. "I don't believe you," I said. "You're testing me."

"Think a minute, Knute. Why would anyone drop a quarter-million-dollar retainer on us just because she called Booth Protection Services instead of the police or the FBI?"

"She's upset. She feels guilty because if she'd called the police, they might have saved his life."

"I wonder why she didn't."

"You don't believe her explanation?"

"Did you?"

"Certainly."

Ashley shook his head. "My dear Knute, I suspect her pretty face has caused you to lose your professional objectivity. If I didn't know you were a happily married man, I'd say you're in love with Ellen. How would you like to take a trip to Lebanon this week? I heard there's a lull in the fighting right now. Take Mamie. She can visit the Holy Land while you find out about the death of Ellen's first husband. But be quiet. I don't want the police to learn what we're up to."

I told Ashley I couldn't imagine what a trip to Beirut would uncover, but he insisted, so I ordered tickets and told Mamie to pack our clothes because we were going to the Holy Land. She was ecstatic; it was the dream of her lifetime. When we reached Tel Aviv, I sent her on a tour of the shrines of Israel, and I continued on to Beirut.

Even though I had seen many videotapes of the fighting and devastation in Beirut, the sight of countless buildings reduced to little more than their frames and of streets clogged with glass, concrete, and twisted steel made me think I was in Berlin in 1945. More amazing to me was the fact that people continued to live, love, and carry on business in the middle of this no-man's land. Although the fighting had abated in the past month, the thumps of mortar shells continued with the regularity of the ticking of a grandfather clock. The concierge at my hotel assured me that the artillery barrages had no mortal intent and that the "boys were just keeping in practice in case the fighting heated up again."

Nevertheless, the backdrop of blasts and falling rubble distracted me day and night. When a shell hit the apartment building behind my hotel, I resolved to complete my business and leave Beirut as fast as duty to my client and to Ashley permitted.

I had no idea how to locate Ellen's friend, Nikos Callimachus. There hadn't been a phone book printed in Beirut for at least five years, probably because most of the phone lines were down. The old books listed no one with his name. The information officer at the American Embassy pretended he had never heard of a Nikos Callimachus, but I knew he was lying by the way his eyes shifted to a person sitting in a glass booth across the hall. When he left to answer a page, I thumbed through his address book and found a listing for a Nikos Callimachus. The spaces for his phone number and address were marked with a big "C," which I assumed meant "confidential."

After three days of running down false leads and meeting blank stares, I assumed that Nikos must have heard by now that I was looking for him. In preparation for my trip I had made a quick study of Middle Eastern mores and learned that, if you want to see someone, you broadcast your intentions and wait until he comes to see you. I parked myself at a table of a sidewalk cafe, ordered a cup of the vile concoction they call coffee, opened up a book of crossword puzzles, and waited.

After a few hours, a handsome young man with mideastern features sat down beside me and asked me in fluent English marked by long vowel sounds and liquid consonants if I were an American. He seemed delighted when I confirmed that I was and volunteered that he had a cousin in New York. After a speech full of tributes to my country, he asked if there were any places I would like to visit in his small and backward land.

"Sir," I said, "I humbly thank you. I would be deeply honored to visit whatever sights you might be so kind as to recommend in your beautiful and historic nation. I must admit, however, that the chief purpose of my trip is to make the acquaintance of a Mr Nikos Callimachus, who is not only a very distinguished citizen of this country, but also a good friend of my employer, Mrs Ellen Stuart, now Mrs Ellen Strafford. Permit me to give you my business card."

He glanced at the card. "You want to meet Mr Callimachus? What an amazing coincidence! I am just on my way to see him now! I will be glad to tell him of your desire, Mr Olsen. Undoubtedly he will be honored by your visit. Would it possible for you to be here tomorrow at the same time?"

I told him that it would be my pleasure to sit at this table all day if it should please Mr Callimachus to join me.

Whatever else people may say about the businessmen of Lebanon, they are, in their way, very efficient. The next day, a few minutes after ten, a tall, graying man of commanding appearance sat down beside me. Three young men sat around us holding Uzis on their laps with practiced ease. I prompted myself to make no sudden movements and said in a cordial tone of voice, "Mr Callimachus, I presume."

He smiled graciously. "How may this citizen of a poor country help our distinguished visitor from the United States?"

After a lengthy speech about the honor his presence conferred upon an unworthy American, I told him that I was acting for a mutual friend, Ellen Pym Stuart, now Ellen Strafford, and wanted to learn, if he had the time and the inclination, what he recalled about the death of Charles Stuart in 1976.

Nikos touched his hand to his eyes and said, "I will never forget that tragic day. I lost then a dear friend, Mr Olsen, and the memory still haunts my dreams. I keep asking myself what I could have done that I failed to do."

He insisted that I spend the afternoon with him on his "little boat," which turned out to be a yacht the size of a U.S. Navy frigate. He treated me to an excellent five-course French dinner with vintage wines. As I ate, he told me fascinating stories of the Mideast never covered by our newspapers. Nikos could not have shown me greater hospitality than if I had been President Carter himself.

He corroborated everything Ellen had said to us. In fact, as I compared the notes I had taken of our conference with Ellen with the notes of my conversations with Nikos, I was impressed by the fact that there was not one factual discrepancy. I couldn't wait to disprove Ashley's suspicions of Ellen.

On my return to San Francisco, the following item appeared on the first page of the *Chronicle:*

POLICE PUZZLES PERSIST;
STRAFFORD STORY A STUMPER;
NO BREAK IN BUZZ BOMBING

Police are still pursuing all possible leads in the mystery slaying of Thomas Wentworth ("Buzz") Strafford, according to Rollie Rupert, the detective in charge of the case.

The explosion was the work of a person well-acquainted with timing mechanisms, Rupert said. The detonator was an inertial counter which set off a charge when Strafford's vehicle had traveled a predetermined distance. A puzzling aspect of the case was the size of the charge.

"It was two or three times bigger than needed to kill the occupants of the vehicle, assuming that was the intent," Rupert said.

The explosive was LN4601, a new and extremely compact formulation. "A charge the size of a fist could blow open the doors of Fort Knox," Rupert added.

I clipped the article and laid it on Ashley's desk. "What do you make of this?" I asked.

"It doesn't look good for our client, does it?"

"What do you mean?"

He waved me to a chair. Instead of responding to my question, he held up the memorandum I had written about my conversation with Nikos Callimachus. "What do you make of his story?" he asked.

"It affirms everything Ellen told us."

"Did you notice that his story matched hers almost word for word?"

"Yes, I'm sure every detail was burned forever into the memories of both of them."

"It's either that, Knute, or they've been refreshing each others' memories recently."

My jaw dropped. "Do you think she—"

Ashley shook his head. "I haven't come to any conclusions yet, but there are a lot of questions we need to answer."

"Such as?"

"Like, who is this Nikos Callimachus?"

"As I said in my memo, Ashley, he's a well-known businessman, an importer. He seems to be friendly with all the factions in Lebanon."

"So what does he import that makes him so popular?"

"He didn't say."

"I think, Knute, it has to be either liquor or guns. If he has a *lot* of money, I bet it's guns."

"Judging by his guards and the size of his yacht, he's loaded. So what does this have to do with Ellen?"

I need to explain at this point why two defense lawyers would, in effect, build a case against their client. Many people, even some lawyers, think a defense attorney takes his retainer and does nothing more until the trial, when he befuddles the state's witnesses with an artful cross-examination that explodes their credibility.

The fact is, the state has hundreds of experts and access to thousands of records not readily available to the defense team. To match its resources, the defense must work around the clock, checking and rechecking all its assumptions, so as to leave no relevant detail unexamined. Although the Rules of Criminal Procedure permit the defense to inspect all the evidence possessed by the state, prosecuting attorneys sometimes "forget" to disgorge some piece of evidence or discover it "just hours" before the trial. *ANTICIPATE, SUSPECT, AND PREPARE* would be Rules inscribed in the John Marshall Conference Room of Blackwood & Associates, except they are so obvious that no one needs to state them.

Ashley asked me to explain the implications of the fact that Ellen's friend, Nikos Callimachus, appeared to be an arms supplier.

"I don't see anything sinister about that," I said. "Gun-running is a respectable business in Beirut. Ellen and Chuck knew all sorts of people there, and isn't hard to believe that Nikos would want to assist a beautiful woman."

"Something strikes me as very odd," Ashley said. "With all his contacts, why didn't Nikos try to negotiate with the kidnappers?" This thought had never occurred to me. Ashley went on, "And maybe the rescue party he put together with his police contact wasn't all that motivated."

My lungs felt as if they were in the grip of Minnesota's sub-zero cold. "Are you saying that the abduction was a front Ellen and Nikos put up to cover the murder of Charles? I can't believe that lovely woman is a murderess. And why would he help her?"

Ashley put an arm around my shoulder. "Knute," he said, "I think you're a bit worn out from your trip. Why don't you take the rest of the day off?"

"No, Ashley, absolutely not. Work's my only restorative. I'll be all right. It's just a shock." I had my secretary bring in a cup of coffee and soon recovered. "I suppose the state has all her phone records by now," I said. "Do you think she was dumb enough to call Nikos?"

"I doubt it, but let's not jump to any conclusions yet. Remember, Knute, we're just speculating."

"Should we call Ellen in and confront her?"

"You mean ask her 'to tell the truth, the whole truth, and nothing but the truth?' Why would we want to do that, Knute? It could be very damaging."

He was right, of course. I don't know why I suggested it. Maybe I wanted Ellen to disprove all our theories or apologize or promise she'd never commit another crime.

"We better find out how she spends her money," Ashley said. "Tell her to come in and sign complete powers of attorney. Make sure they cover her holdings everywhere. Better get them in Arabic and French, too, plus whatever languages they speak in Switzerland. And get them notarized by all the consuls."

I suspected Ellen would not be pleased when she learned we wanted to investigate her financial affairs.

"What is this?" she said when I called her. "Do you suspect me of murdering my husband?"

"No, Mrs Strafford," I said. "Our job is to anticipate any evidence the state may produce. We have to plan how to keep it out, or, at the very least, blunt its impact."

"I find it quite interesting that the state doesn't consider me a suspect, but my lawyers do. Need I remind you, Mr Olsen, that I hired you for the sole purpose of explaining to Rollie Rupert why I called Booth Protection Services rather than the FBI or his parking ticket trolls. That's *all* I hired you for." With that she slammed down the phone.

41

Her attitude changed dramatically when the *Examiner* reported on October 14:

STRAFFORD WIDOW INDICTED; ACCUSED OF MURDERING HUSBAND AND CHAUFFEUR

Ellen Strafford, widow of the late Thomas W. ("Buzz") Strafford, was indicted yesterday on charges of first-degree murder in the death of her husband and his chauffeur, Juan Fangio, on August 21. Both men were killed by a car bomb.

It appeared that Mrs Strafford had acted alone, said Rollie Rupert, the detective in charge of the case. He cautioned, however, that police had not yet completed their investigation.

Mrs Strafford's first husband, Charles Stuart, was murdered by Lebanese terrorists in 1976. Rupert said his death was not being investigated. "There would be no point in that," he said. "The crime occurred in Lebanon, and it is a matter for the Lebanese police, or whatever authorities they still have over there."

Mrs Strafford's arraignment will take place before Judge E. Ray Tompkins. It is rumored that Ashley Blackwood, the well-known San Francisco criminal attorney, will represent Mrs Strafford. Mr Blackwood had no comment.

Imogene Cato of the *Examiner* had a note in her gossip column:

Friends and neighbors of Mrs Strafford were incredulous when they heard of her indictment for murder.

Diana Duke, wife of industrialist Donald Duke, said, "I simply can't believe it. Everybody loves her. She gives the most wonderful dinner parties and has such exquisite taste. I'm sure the police have made a terrible mistake."

At the arraignment Ellen posted two million dollars bail and delivered the powers of attorney I had requested. When I told Ashley of their receipt, he said, "Call home and have Mamie pack your bags."

"Beirut again?"

He nodded.

Within a week, despite the evasions of Swiss bankers and the incompetence of the Lebanese bureaucracy, I had collected enough information to call Ashley from Beirut. "Guess where Ellen's money has been going?" I asked.

"Some Islamic organization?"

"How did you know?" Ashley's insight never failed to amaze me. "It's the Tower of Allah."

"What in the hell is the 'Tower of Allah?'"

"A splinter group of the True Sons of Allah, as far as I can figure. They say they're purifying the world in anticipation of the return of Mohammed. The word is that they're a heavily armed and well-disciplined bunch of murderers."

"And Nikos Callimachus is one of their chiefs."

"How did you know that?"

"I didn't. It was just a guess."

"Do you think there's something in that we can use?"

"Hell, no, Knute. We don't want the jury to know that

her first husband's money went to a Muslim 'death squad,' especially if any of the jury are Jewish."

A paralegal in our office had researched Ellen's relationship with both her husbands. On the surface the marriages had been amicable, with no hint of infidelity or disagreement on money matters.

"Do you think she killed them just for their estates?" I asked Ashley. "I can't believe she's that cold-blooded."

"The answer has to be in Beirut, Knute. Remember, half her family was back there."

I told Ashley that, even though detective Rupert had never heard of them, inertial timing devices were as plentiful in Lebanon as gold watches, but the Chief was right that the explosive charge was too big for the job. Apparently the manufacturer had introduced a new explosive with a number similar to the old, and there had been a few casualties here and there because of inadequate labeling.

"That could explain her broken arm," I said. "She didn't fall off Muffin. She wanted to watch and stood too close. The blast knocked her down."

"Right, Knute. Muffin didn't rear up. The state's vet says Muffin is almost totally deaf."

"So we have our work cut out for us—right?"

That was the understatement of my lifetime. The prosecutors now had the means and the motive, and we had an uncooperative client. When I asked Ashley if he planned to bargain a plea, he said he'd discuss it with Ellen when she came in tomorrow.

Our interview with her the next day proved that a determined woman is more than a match for any man, be he a Caesar or a Bonaparte. Ashley summed up the case against her as he thought the prosecution would make it appear. "The state can show that you had a motive—money—and access to the means—Nikos Callimachus—and they can knock out your riding alibi. From the way it looks right now, it will be difficult to break their case."

Ellen looked at Ashley with what, in any other woman, would be called a sneer. "Are you really that weak? Do you try only the cases you are sure to win? Is that the kind of attorney you are?"

Ashley didn't respond to her assault. He explained once more the links in the prosecution's case and invited her to provide him with any information which might break or weaken them.

She said, "Mr Blackwood, that is *your* job, and I expect you to do it well. You are being generously compensated. You have a reputation which will be blackened by losing a case that will appear on the front page of every newspaper in three continents. Although you have not yet asked me, under no circumstance will I consent to a plea which would prevent the completion of my life's work."

"Which is?"

She stood up suddenly, raised her right hand, and cried in a voice that dripped blood, "Vengeance! I will not rest until I have seen the severed heads of every one of the Rashad clan, down to the tiniest infant. This I have sworn on the grave of my grandfather, Mahmet Arazi, in retribution for his murder and the murder of his children and grandchildren."

I sat in a state of shock, afraid that any word I said might encompass me within her vow of revenge. Ashley's jaw dropped, but he quickly composed his features and said he accepted her decision and would try the case to the best of his ability. If, however, she had any doubts about his competence, she should discharge him now so as to leave her next counsel time to prepare.

Ellen drew in her breath, exhaled, and said with a warm, confiding tone of voice, "Mr Blackwood, I do not doubt your competence. You have assured me that you will put forth your best efforts on my behalf. That is all I want." With that our meeting ended.

After she left, Ashley and I looked at each other over the conference table. "Well," he said, "we better think of something."

The next day he called Ellen into the office again. I was surprised he didn't ask me to be present, since I always made notes for his use on direct examination. He said, "Not this time, Knute. I think she'll open up more if the two of us talk alone." He must have judged correctly, because they talked all day and, when they finished, Ashley said he was pleased with the results.

The trial commenced on March 8, 1982. The media could not have given more fanfare to the arrival of a delegation from the Andromeda galaxy. The words Strafford, Blackwood, and Ted Dewey, the prosecutor, appeared on the front page of every newspaper in the country for a month. Multi-page biographies of the three of them and of Ellen and her two husbands appeared in the Sunday supplements and the weekly magazines. Information, however sketchy or unreliable, about Ellen and her husbands became the Holy Grail of the media. Reporters, photographers, and television crews tramped around her house until the lawn and garden looked like the no-man's land around Verdun in 1918. A television station offered a reward of $10,000 to anyone who could provide the location of Ellen's apartment. At the commencement of the trial, crowds packed the streets around the Hall of Justice.

Ashley and I agreed that, to the extent possible, we should choose jurors with middle-class values, since lower-class jurors would share a hang-the-rich mentality, and upper-class jurors would have no mercy towards a woman who had killed one of their own. Middle-class jurors, on the other hand, might applaud the resourcefulness of a woman who rose to the top ranks, never mind how. With a few exceptions, we succeeded in obtaining the kind of jury we wanted.

Ted Dewey, the prosecuting attorney, did a creditable job of putting in the state's case. He walked his experts at a comfortable pace through a description of the murder scene, allowed them the time they needed to explain the explosives and the inertial timing device, and showed through a dramatic reconstruction—which we attempted unsuccessfully to exclude—how the blast wave would have knocked down anyone within a quarter mile with enough force to break a bone, and how the X rays of Ellen's broken arm were consistent with the type of break shown in the reconstruction. He introduced tapes and transcripts of Ellen's phone calls to the police and the statements she had made to them about her fall from Muffin; put on an expert to testify to Muffin's hearing impairment; and showed Ellen's links to Nikos Callimachus, the funds she had dispatched to his group, and his access to explosives and detonators.

Although Ted built a strong case for the prosecution, he made a serious mistake when, referring to Nikos, he brought up the kidnapping and murder of Charles Stuart, Ellen's first husband. This opened the door for us to introduce at a later time evidence of the Rashad clan's massacre of Ellen's family.

On cross-examination Ashley attacked the state's witnesses with the fury of a lioness protecting her young. He derided the state's reconstruction of the blast, impugned in his best traffic court style the competence of the explosives experts, pointed to suspicious blanks in the telephone taps, scoffed at the suppositions of the state's orthopedist about the manner of Ellen's fall, and made the state's veterinarian admit that Muffin was not so deaf he wouldn't react to an explosion which rocked the neighborhood.

When the prosecution rested, Ashley put on our own experts to counter the testimony of the state's experts. Although they failed to nullify the state's evidence, they presented enough alternative theories to confuse the issue and befuddle the jury.

Still, we had not damaged the state's case sufficiently to have more than an even chance of obtaining an acquittal, and we had to face the issue whether to put Ellen on the stand. I thought, and Ashley concurred, that her physical beauty might sway the men on the jury who stared at her every time she moved a muscle. By the same token, she would alienate every woman on the jury who hadn't yet made up her mind against her.

When we asked her whether she wanted to take the stand, she said, "Gentlemen, I *insist* on taking the stand. You have done all you could do, and I compliment you on your performance, but now it's up to me."

Ashley explained to her that the state's cross-examination might put her in a worse light than she was at present, but she demanded the right to speak in her own defense.

When Ashley called her to the stand, there was an outburst in the courtroom which could be heard a block away. Reporters dashed for the doors to reach the phones in the hall outside the courtroom, and, at the same time, those who were listening to the proceedings in the hallway, attempted to push their way into the courtroom. Judge Tompkins pounded his gavel like a blacksmith and grew hoarse shouting for order. It was several minutes before a degree of quiet returned, but only a degree.

When Ellen rose and took the stand, silence blanketed the courtroom. The bleached oak wainscoting of Department 23, the plywood seats, the grimy concrete floors metamorphosed into a cathedral of justice. Time stopped. The world outside ceased to exist.

After saying "I do" in a firm and musical voice, Ellen arranged herself on the witness chair, crossed her legs, and smiled at the judge and jury.

Ashley ran through a series of questions to identify her for the record and asked her whether she wanted to respond to the accusations made by the prosecution.

"I most certainly do," she said. As she spoke, she leaned forward in the witness box, and the jury leaned forward with her as if on the same string. A good sign, I thought.

Ashley asked her to describe her youth in Lebanon and how the Rashad family had murdered her grandfather and all the Arazi family but her when she was a girl of twelve. Ted Dewey objected on the grounds of relevance, but Ashley pointed out that Mr Dewey had opened up the issue earlier by referring to the murder of Ellen's first husband in Lebanon. As a result, he contended, defendant was entitled to clear up any misunderstandings in the minds of the jury about the effect of the factional fighting in Lebanon on her family. Ted's objection was overruled. He ground his molars audibly as he walked away from the bench.

Ellen spoke of the terror which had been inflicted on her family by the insensate blood lust of the Mideast. It had left her with a lifelong fear of violence, she said, to the point that she seldom read a newspaper and never watched television.

It was a moving account. Ashley's voice choked as he concluded by asking her for the names and ages of all in her family who had been massacred. Several jurors wiped their eyes as she read the list. I had difficulty repressing my own tears.

Ellen's voice changed from grief to breathless lyricism

as she described the rebirth of hope she experienced when she married "Buzz" Strafford. Their best times, she said, came during the trips they took for the Red Cross, ferrying supplies on their yacht to towns in the Andes devastated by volcanoes, to villages in Guatemala decimated by partisan vendettas, and to malnourished orphans in the barrios of Rio de Janeiro. Just before Buzz's last day, they had escrowed with their bankers a 100-million-dollar challenge grant for the relief of refugees from Nicaragua and had finalized their plans for a six-month fund-raising tour of the United States.

"At the happiest moment of Buzz's life," she said, "when he had finally found the destined use for his millions, some assassin cut him down and ended my happiness forever."

As she spoke these words, I saw that the jurors could no longer hold back their tears. Judge Tompkins called a ten-minute recess to give them time to recover. After the recess, Ashley asked Ellen a few more questions about the scope of the relief they brought to the victims of poverty, volcanism, and violence.

As he spoke I sensed that another volcano was at the point of eruption at the prosecutor's table. Ted Dewey looked as if he wanted to jump from his seat and shout, "It's a pack of lies," but caution made him smolder in place. No doubt he feared alienating the jury by scoffing at Ellen's tragic story.

When Ashley finished, Ellen started to rise from the witness box, but the court cautioned her that the prosecution was entitled to cross-examine her. She nodded at the judge and said in a tone a queen might use in permitting a subject to address her, "Very well then, let them proceed."

On cross-examination, Ted challenged her to point to any public statement she or her husband had made prior to his death regarding the "so-called" 100-million-dollar matching grant, or, for that matter, any of their "alleged" work for the Red Cross. Through the testimony of lawyers, trust officers, accountants, and probate clerks, he cemented in the jury's mind the fact that Ellen would inherit about 200 million dollars from Buzz Strafford's estate.

On re-direct examination by Ashley, Ellen stated that the money she would inherit resulted not from Buzz's will, but from an antenuptial agreement which governed the provisions of both their wills. The grant to the foundation had been executed but was not to be publicized, she said, until the foundation had prepared a publicity campaign. Now, as a result of his death, she doubted that it could be carried out on the scale he had intended.

"Buzz," she said, "was terribly anxious to launch the campaign. You see, he had a history of heart trouble. Two weeks before his death, his doctors advised him to undergo a triple coronary bypass. All he lived for during his last weeks on earth was to leave behind an institution that would alleviate the sufferings of those whom society had ignored."

Ashley recalled to the stand the state's explosives expert and made him admit that the explosive devices which had been used were very sensitive, that even men with extensive experience were killed by accidental blasts, and that it was highly unlikely an amateur would have the knowledge required to rig a device of the sort used in this case.

On the issue of Ellen's inheritance, Ashley brought out the fact that before Buzz's death Ellen held in her own name assets in excess of fifty million dollars, which she had inherited from her father and first husband. To the dismay of prosecutor Dewey, Ashley produced for corroboration a medical history of Buzz's heart condition that had eluded the state's search. Muffin became the subject of the conflicting opinions of several veterinarians on the degree of his hearing impairment until the mention of Muffin brought laughter from the gallery.

Back and forth it went for weeks. One day popular opinion favored an acquittal, the next day a conviction.

After two months, the time arrived for closing arguments. Ted Dewey made a reasoned but uninspiring argument from the evidence. When he finished, Ashley rose to his feet and began, as he always did, by complimenting the jury on their patience, intelligence, and patriotism, saying, "Few jurors have had to sit as long as you have and hear such confusing and conflicting testimony as you have heard. So you must wonder at times, 'Is this a movie, or is this real life?' I have often asked myself the same question. Alfred Hitchcock in his prime could not have constructed a thriller with more shadows and surprises than this trial has produced over the last two months.

"The state contends that Mrs Strafford assembled an

explosive device using technology unavailable in the U.S. and, until this trial, unknown to the forensics unit of California's Department of Justice. The most sophisticated criminal laboratory in the country had never seen the type of timing device the state contends Mrs Strafford attached to her husband's car. Where was she supposed to obtain a device unknown to all of California's experts? Assuming she had such a device, how could she, a woman untrained in explosives, assemble and arm it without blowing herself up? And why would a wealthy, beautiful, and charming woman hazard death solely to add some of her husband's millions to her own millions?

"What motive could she have?" he asked. "What advantage could she obtain? She had no children, no family. She couldn't possibly spend it all on herself. All she could do with it was increase her already lavish donations to charity. Ladies and gentlemen of the jury, I submit that only a person seriously deranged would undertake such huge perils for a purely charitable purpose.

"Mrs Strafford has been in the same room with you for two months now. You have had the opportunity to observe her for nearly seven hours each day. She was on the stand for two days. Did she seem consumed by a thirst for her husband's blood? Did she seem mad enough to risk her life in order to add to her considerable fortune? Of course not, but that is exactly what the prosecution claims. Step back and study the state's case. You will find no proof of either means or motivation. It simply doesn't add up!

"But, ladies and gentlemen, let me give you an account which does add up. You remember that every man, woman, and child of Mrs Strafford's very distinguished family in Lebanon, everyone but Mrs Strafford, was murdered by members of the Rashad family when she was a child of twelve. Only she escaped the holocaust. How does that tragedy bear on our case? Remember that her first husband, Charles Stuart, who went to Lebanon in the cause of peace, was murdered by a group whose identity was never established.

"Fact one, murder of her family by a mideastern gang.

"Fact two, murder of her first husband by a mideastern gang.

"Fact three, the experts from California's crime lab admit that the timing device used to set off the charge that took the life of Buzz Strafford must have come from the Mideast, where it had been used frequently to take the lives of many innocent men, women, and children.

"Fact four, the prosecution's own witnesses admit that only an expert well-trained in handling explosives could successfully assemble a device of this sort. And where are such experts located? The Mideast.

"Now, what does the prosecution make of facts one, two, three, and four? That somebody from the Mideast, possibly the same group that wiped out Mrs Strafford's family and kidnapped and murdered her first husband, came to California and tried to extort millions from her second husband, then, when they failed, set a bomb to blow him up? That's what you and I would conclude after thinking about facts one, two, three, and four, but not the prosecution.

"Maybe I'm not as smart as Mr Dewey, but from these four facts, *I* would never come to the conclusion that Mrs Strafford perpetrated such a hideous crime. No, I'd look around and see who had both a *motive* to do it and the *skill* to carry it out. I don't, for the life of me, know why detective Rupert never sat down and said to his officers, 'Look, some mideast gang kidnapped her first husband and demanded ransom. When it wasn't paid, they killed him. Now her second husband gets notes threatening death unless he gives them two million dollars. He doesn't pay and he gets blown up. Looks like the same gang to me.'

"Maybe that line of thinking seems too easy, too obvious for clever investigators like detective Rupert and his men. But to me, it makes a lot of sense.

"Ladies and gentlemen of the jury, the only reasonable conclusion you can draw from the evidence is that the perpetrators of this vicious crime are not in this courtroom today. They sit far away, sip black coffee under a hot sun with AK-47's cradled on their laps, and laugh at our proceedings."

I watched the faces of the lawyers at the prosecutor's table as Ashley summed up to the jury. As he began, they wore expressions of amused interest, as if anticipating a good story. Soon concern erased their smiles, fear appeared, then anger, and finally rage. I half-expected

Dewey to leap up and throttle Ashley until he agreed to take back every word.

Dewey glowed with anger when Ashley ended, and he let his emotions run away with him in his rebuttal argument. It is an effect Ashley produces by design. Ted was a capable prosecutor, but in making his rebuttal, he spoke too fast and with too much heat to persuade the jury to his point of view. He stooped to ridicule in countering Ashley's suggestion that a mideast death squad was responsible for Mr Strafford's death. He lost the jury's sympathy when he called Ellen a "charter member of the liar-of-the-month club." The case might have gone the other way if Ted had requested a recess and let his temper cool until the next morning. On such small matters do great trials often hang.

While the jury deliberated, Ellen sat in the office with Ashley and me. Though her stress was great, she engaged us in a discussion about the history of English law. She complimented me on my investigation and Ashley on his presentation. She said that if the decision were to go against her, she would still feel that her lawyers had done all that they could.

It may seem strange to say it, but the two days she sat with us while awaiting the jury's verdict were the happiest days in my life. Never before or since have I been in the presence of such a beautiful and thoughtful woman, except for my wife. When the jury came in with a verdict of "not guilty," I was saddened to think that I would never see her again. I thought of Ellen five years later when we defended Ramona Krafft on a charge of mayhem. What a world of difference between the refinement of an Ellen and the overt sensuality of a Ramona!

The day after her acquittal, Ellen left for a new home in France. From there she wired Ashley an additional $250,000 to close out her account. He told me he had never requested more than the original retainer, but he was glad to have it. Ellen's case was his most expensive trial to date.

That Saturday as Ashley, his friend Alexia, Mamie, and I sipped champagne at the *Top of the Mark*, I asked Ashley what Rule he derived from the Strafford case. He thought a minute and said, "*IF YOU HAVE A SYMPATHETIC CLIENT, COME UP WITH ANOTHER MURDERER, PREFERABLY ONE FARAWAY.*"

"Explain that," I said.

"Knute, the jury doesn't like to send an attractive woman to the gas chamber. They sit in the same room with her and the judge and the attorneys for two months. We all become part of one big family. So if you can provide a half-way plausible story that somebody else did it, the jurors will be happy to let your client go. The jury won't make a hard decision if you can give it an easy way out."

I started writing this biography a year after Ashley's untimely death and felt the need to do additional background research in Lebanon. While Mamie revisited the Holy Land, I went to Beirut to meet the American ambassador to Lebanon. I asked him whether Ellen might be in danger from her old enemies, the Rashad clan.

He shook his head. "I doubt it. I knew something about them years ago, but they're all dead now. Every last one of them, from patriarchs to infants, has been killed off, one by one."

I asked him if he knew who had done the killing. He said he didn't, but, if he did, he would make a point of forgetting. "All I can say is, they did quite a job. Every last Rashad in the two hemispheres was tracked down and killed. It must have cost somebody a fortune."

THREE

Although I have documented two of Ashley's legal victories, I have shown only a glimpse of him in his personal life. His views on criminal law, his relationships with his parents and his girl friend, Alexia, and his fateful high school romance, evidence a profound, multi-faceted personality.

Ashley's critics contend that he had no life outside the courtroom. Imogene Cato of the *San Francisco Examiner,* for example, wrote that Ashley expended all his energies trying cases, so that his social intercourse "consisted of discussing the weather with his lackeys."

Nothing could be further from the truth. Ashley had an extensive acquaintance with the highest levels of San Francisco society. He received invitations to all the prestigious charitable events, and, when time permitted him to attend, the social columns invariably noted his presence the next day. As I thumb through his scrap book, I am reminded that a local magazine, much to Ashley's amusement, listed him for years as one of San Francisco's "ten most eligible bachelors" and speculated which of its "ten most eligible bachelorettes" might form a partnership with him.

Far from limiting himself to "discussing the weather with his lackeys," Ashley met with his associates every Thursday evening at a restaurant near our office. Although we spent most of our time discussing the status of active cases and evaluating new ones, Ashley made sure to leave time at the end of the evening for a few minutes of personal chitchat about our families. If he was in an expansive mood, he treated us to some hilarious anecdotes of his successful trials. He was such a good storyteller that we all laughed, even if we had heard them before.

The highlight of the office year was our Mexican Christmas fiesta. The staff festooned the office with balloons, piñatas, and red, white, and green crêpe paper. Ashley loaded the conference tables with burritos, enchiladas, fajitas, and pitchers of margaritas, tequilas, and cerveza. No discussion of client matters was permitted. The evening was all food, drink, and lively banter. The party reached its climax at midnight when Ashley announced the amount of our bonuses for the year and handed out checks to all of us, thus heightening the evening's *bonhommie.* We proposed humorous toasts to him, and he responded with a gracious speech thanking us for our efforts during the year. When the party ended, he made certain each employee had a cab or a designated driver for a safe return home.

At least once a year he honored my wife Mamie and me by inviting us to a private dinner with his constant companion, Alexia Capri, a gorgeous fashion model. Ashley never dwelled on trivial matters, such as the weather or a bout with the flu. He discussed topics of national interest, like defense spending, the space program, or the state of the arts. When Mamie and I returned from these evenings, we marveled at the cordiality of our host and the lofty level of his conversation. Mamie, like me, grew up on Minnesota's Iron Range, but, during the three years she worked as an executive secretary at General Mills, she met many of the political and business leaders of the country. My seven years at the University of Minnesota's College of Liberal Arts and its Law School familiarized me with the works of writers of all times and places. Mamie and I agreed, however, that no one we had ever met approached Ashley's reach and sophistication.

Most Twin Citians regard emigreés from the Range as a species of humanity distinguishable from *homo sapiens* by the oddity of their speech patterns and their attachment to hockey and binge drinking. Ashley, however, treated me as his peer in culture and intellectual attainment. He sensed that I embraced his values and respected his abilities. He appreciated my Iron Range common sense and my trove of "Ole and Lena" jokes, which never failed to relieve his mind of the stresses of the courtroom.

He once confided that, although I was not the most qualified candidate for associate, my Minnesota background, my unusual name, and my sense of humor had led him to hire me. He explained that his father, Herbert, was a devoted football fan, just like my father. But for his mother's opposition, Ashley said, Herb would have named him "Bernie Bierman Blackwood" in honor of the coach of the victorious Golden Gophers of the 1930s. I was not so fortunate. My mother tried but failed to prevent my father from christening me after Knute Rockne, the famous Notre Dame coach.

Ashley lived comfortably. When I first knew him, he had a town house on Telegraph Hill and owned two cars, the mandatory California convertible and a roomy Rolls-Royce. Later he acquired a cabin in the mountains to escape the jackals of the media. At the time I met him, Ashley's relationship with Alexia Capri was already five years old, and it continued, with brief interruptions, until the date of his untimely death. Some writers who cannot forgive Ashley for his courtroom successes contend that the fact he never married Alexia proves his single-minded devotion to money and legal notoriety. To this charge there are several answers.

Alexia had made it clear to Ashley from their first encounter that she had no desire to give up her privacy and modeling career for marriage and children. She and Ashley defined themselves as "engaged to each other, but with no date set for the wedding."

I often visited with Alexia when she dropped into the office during what Ashley called her "scorched earth" shopping expeditions. She was breathtakingly tall and slim, with a beautifully sculpted face, an aquiline nose, hollow cheeks, and a modest bust, all of which Mamie claimed were crafted by surgery or other artifice. I gave no credence to Mamie's comment. I've known her to be, on more than one occasion, a little critical of especially attractive women.

I once asked Alexia at dinner where she came from and how she happened to take up modeling. She winked and gave me a mischievous smile. "That's a long story," she said and sealed her lips. Ashley took me aside later and whispered that Alexia had lived most of her life in the shadow of tragedy and never discussed her personal history. I apologized to her later and said I hadn't meant to pry into her life. She acknowledged my apology with a charming smile. To show her good will, she confided to me that she came from North Dakota and that her birth name was Flanders.

I asked Mamie whether she'd ever seen Alexia's picture in any of the innumerable fashion magazines which litter our living room. "No," she said, "she isn't the kind of model you see in my magazines." Mamie didn't elaborate on her comment, and I didn't press for an explanation. The world of women's fashions is far beyond my understanding.

There was an even stronger reason for Ashley's persisting in the single state. He told me once over an out-of-town dinner that he had been engaged to his high school sweetheart, Amy Bontemps, during their last two years before graduation. Their engagement terminated with such acrimony on her part that he never again ventured into a formal arrangement with another woman. At their Graduation Ball, Amy had pressed him to set a date for the wedding. It was a topic of special importance to her since—not to put too fine a point upon it—she was pregnant. Ashley believed that another man was the father, but, to avoid embarrassing her, he never pressed the issue.

"We were dancing to the Tennessee Waltz in the high school gym," he said, "when she insisted on my setting a date now and then. I told her we should wait until we'd matured and established ourselves in our careers. Maybe we'd discover after a few years that we had become very different people from what we were in high school. All I wanted, Knute, was to avoid a mistake which would result in unhappiness for us and any children we might have. To be honest, I had relied on her to take the responsibility for avoiding pregnancy, and she let me down.

"I was straightforward with her, but she began to whine and cry and threaten, saying she'd told everyone we were getting married in July. If you can believe it, she threatened to go to the police and tell them all she knew about A&A Social Services!"

At this point, I wanted to ask Ashley what A&A Social Services was, but we were interrupted by a waiter, and it was three years before I learned the true story of this controversial episode of Ashley's life.

"When the waltz ended," Ashley continued, "I walked her outside the gym and said, 'Look, Amy, we've had some good years together and we've made a lot of money from

A&A. A quick trip to a doctor I know and you'll be as clean as any other graduate. But, if you go around spreading a lot of lies, people will laugh in your face and you will only harm yourself.'"

Would that Amy had heeded his advice and never looked back! How many lives would have been spared!

Ashley's true romance was not with Amy or Alexia, but with that jealous mistress, the Law. It was a relationship which severely taxed his health. The years he spent in court softened his features even as they sharpened his mind. Towards the end of his career his mind could mentally strategize more trials than his body could physically endure. In what leisure he had, he read newspapers and some weekly magazines, but no books other than those relating to criminal law. He listened to no music, saw no plays or movies unless in conjunction with some social event. It amazed me that a man who had chosen California as his residence never swam, skied, bicycled, hiked, or camped. Alexia and I conspired to enroll him in a health and fitness program which required three workouts a week under the supervision of a personal trainer, but he seldom adhered to the program for more than a few months at a time.

I once asked him whether he ever felt lonely. He looked at me with a shocked expression and said, "Knute, if you're serious about the law, there isn't time for anything else. When I see opposing counsel looking sleek and tan, I know I've won the case."

He may have been exaggerating, but I made sure not to venture outside without taking measures to avoid being branded by the sun.

Although his victories in the *Tyler* and *Strafford* cases were landmarks in the history of American jurisprudence, Ashley said they were, in economic terms, pyrrhic victories. Even the generous retainers we received from Ellen Strafford failed to raise Blackwood & Associates much above break-even for the years 1981 and 1982. At the end of 1982, the firm's bank account was so low that Ashley had to raid his personal funds to cover the office rent.

A month after the conclusion of the Strafford case, Ashley announced, "It's time now, Knute, to start providing for our futures. Criminal law doesn't pay nowadays unless you're protecting the Mafia, and I promised myself years ago that I would never, for any amount, represent a criminal organization that has brought such grief to the world. We'll focus on personal injury work and won't touch a criminal case for five years. That way we can do the greatest good for the greatest number and provide for our own futures as well. Instead of keeping people out of jail, which is negative justice, we'll obtain fair compensation for their injuries. That's what I call positive justice."

My feelings accorded with his, but Ashley had made the same declaration in the past, only to retract it a few months later when an intriguing case came to his desk. He would rather accept the challenge, whatever the cost to his health or checking account, than live with the thought that he had failed to answer the plea of a victim of Society.

The future is unpredictable. Just when life at Blackwood & Associates had fallen into a comfortable pattern of settling and occasionally trying personal injury cases, Ashley entered my office on October 1, 1982, more agitated than I had ever seen him and handed me the following letter:

September 28, 1982

Ashley,

I suppose you want to forget all about me. But sure as hell I'm not about to forget you, not after what you done to me, damn you.

I'm the little girl you took advantage of in high school. You used me for what I can't bear to think about, you bastard. And then you left me. I wrote off all men until I met my dear husband Edmund.

I read about you in the paper and the case you had for that rich bitch. Some life, Ashley, defending people like that.

Seeing your picture started me crying so hard Ed made me tell him the whole story about how you took advantage of me with your dating service and all the other girls in A&A because we trusted you.

Ed and I talked it over with our lawyer and he said you owe me a LOT. You must be making tons of money out there he said, and you owe me half because California has community property laws, and if we'd been married I'd get half of everything.

I could take you to court and show the world you're no

better than a street pimp. But I'll settle for a million bucks cash which is being real nice and I won't write you any more. But you better pay fast or else I'll sue you for all you got.

Your former fiancée,
Amy Bontemps Mortimer

I winced as I handed the letter back to Ashley. "She's like everybody else. She wants money and then makes up a reason why she should get it. You're not going to answer it, are you?"

"I don't know, Knute."

"I sure wouldn't."

Although I didn't at that time know more than the name of A&A Social Services, I sensed from the tenor of the letter that the writer attributed her current misfortunes to her past business involvement with Ashley. In my experience, it is best to ignore a threatening letter, as any reply only exacerbates the rage of the injured person. Silence is irritating, but a reply dignifies the accusation.

Ashley ignored my advice and wrote the following letter, which I found after his death in his personal correspondence files.

October 6, 1982

My dear Amy,

Your letter brought back memories of persons and places I had long forgotten since my legal practice leaves me little time to contemplate the past.

You say that our A&A venture resulted in your engaging in some acts which demeaned you in some way. If so, your actions were what is known in the Law of Agency as "frolics of your own," actions which are not attributable to the employer since they were not performed in furtherance of the employer's business.

Need I remind you that we were partners, which means that I did not employ you: you were your own employer. What you did beyond the scope of our dating service is your concern, not mine. If you engaged in any salacious acts, it was by your choice. Whatever you gained as a result, was and is your property, and I make no claim to my partnership share of the proceeds.

I also remind you that A&A received awards from the Jaycees and the governor's office for excellence in youthful enterprise. Such honors would not have been awarded if there had been the least suspicion that the enterprise condoned acts of moral turpitude.

In short, I fail to see your point in bringing up at this date your extralegal activities.

Your claim that you are entitled to compensation on the basis that I breached a promise of marriage is outrageous, especially coming from a person who was pregnant by another man. I assume that your claim, if you had one, would arise under Minnesota law. Let me inform you that (a) claims for breach of contract of marriage were outlawed long ago by Minnesota Laws, Sections 550.01 to 553.03, and (b) at any event, the six-year statute of limitations for contract actions under Minnesota Laws, Section 541.05, Subd. 1(1), has long since barred any action on your part.

I hope this reply will cause you to reconsider your frivolous and unwarranted claims. If you persist, I assure you that you will be sued for defamation of character, and I will call the matter to the attention of the district attorney.

I trust this letter finds you and your husband in good health.

Yours truly,

Ashley

Although Ashley's response was justified by the facts, it was, in my opinion, very impolitic. I can imagine the recipient brooding over the cold, legal tone of the letter, a tone completely at variance with Ashley's normally considerate and gracious manner. Yet the reader must put himself in his shoes and consider the provocation.

A happy event took place in November of the same year when Ashley invited his parents to San Francisco for a week's vacation. They had never traveled beyond Minnesota, and Ashley thought they would enjoy a week of sight-seeing on the West Coast. His greatest problem was convincing them to fly. Neither of them had been inside an airplane and both felt that flying over the Rocky Mountains was tempting Providence. Travel by car or train from Minneapolis to California and back was impractical, since it would have left them only a day or two to spend with Ashley. Convincing them to fly took more effort, Ashley said, than inducing a jury to acquit a confessed murderer. But succeed he did, and they arrived safely in San Francisco, congratulating themselves that they had cheated certain death.

As soon as they unpacked, they made Ashley show

them all the sights of San Francisco. The three of them raced around the city as if it were going to sink under the waters of the Pacific at midnight like the village in the old German tale. By 2 A.M. Ashley felt as if he had been on a twenty-mile forced march.

The next morning Herb and Adele were eager to drive down to Los Angeles for a tour of the homes of the stars, shopping along the Mexican border, visiting the national parks, and returning the same night. They were incredulous when Ashley told them that their plan involved a trip of some five hundred miles each way.

Ashley packed his bag, and for seven days drove them through southern California, northern Mexico, and western Nevada, stopping at every tourist attraction along the way. He said it was like riding a rocket to the planets of the solar system in one week. After Herb and Adele left, he spent a day in bed.

I hoped that Ashley would invite me to meet his parents, and I was not disappointed. He planned that we would all have dinner together, but, since his parents' must-see list included a musical that started at 7:30, we had time only for a cocktail before they set off for Geary Street.

Herbert was an imposing figure: six feet three, shoulders like an ox, thighs like tree trunks, and fists the size of a catcher's mitt. His expression had the intensity of a boxer probing for an opportunity to land an uppercut to the chin. His conversational topics consisted solely of sports and taxes. Because of his booming voice, I found it difficult to express my opinions in his presence.

Adele was of medium height with a good figure and attractive face, but she lacked Herb's vivid personality. In his presence, her voice was flat, her face devoid of expression, and she volunteered no word of conversation. In later years when I spoke to her privately, I found she had a fertile and penetrating mind and was remarkably well-read for a person who had never attended college.

Our cocktail conversation took an unexpected turn. Herb and Adele had read about the *Strafford* case, but had never connected Ashley to it. "Son, what kind of lawyer would defend a woman who killed two husbands?" Herb asked. "Why would anybody want to set her free to kill again?"

That question is the curse of the criminal bar. Complete strangers come up to me at a party and dare me to justify my livelihood, never considering that, if I asked them to enumerate their contributions towards the betterment of the human condition, they would be insulted at my effrontery. So, when someone poses that question to me, I smile and say, "Hey, it's a living." If the questioner persists, I excuse myself and walk away.

Most lawyers make the mistake of answering with the simplistic formulation that "Every man is innocent until proven guilty," to which the questioner always replies, "But if you believe he's guilty, how can you in all conscience defend him?" Having trapped himself, all the lawyer can say is, "That's the law."

Ashley, however, wished to make a meaningful response to his father. He went into his "trance" state to formulate an answer that would reassure his mother and father that his work did honor to the Blackwood name.

"Mother," he began as he emerged from his contemplation, "I want to tell you that I was the lawyer who obtained the acquittal of Ellen Strafford."

At these words Herb and Adele's eyes widened and their mouths sagged open. They said, nearly in unison, "*You* were her lawyer?"

"Yes, and I'm proud of it. And I'm proud of a legal system where the state carries the burden of proving the defendant's guilt, because the defendant is presumed innocent. Not only that, it has to prove guilt beyond a reasonable doubt, and the jury has to reach a unanimous verdict. Don't you agree that this is the way it ought to be?"

"Not in that Strafford woman's case," Herb said. "I read the newspapers and watched television, and she looked guilty as hell. How could you stand there and tell the jury she was innocent? Why should she get the benefit of the doubt?"

"Because the prosecution has all the power of the state on its side. It has the police, the FBI, and the district attorney's office. It has access to all the phone records, the vital statistics, the labs, the phone traces, wiretaps— you name it. The state gets the first shot at the story, and you can bet it tells the newspapers everything that suggests the defendant did it and leaves out everything that hints that maybe he didn't do it. The state has a case all put together by the time the defendant has called a lawyer."

"But, Ashley," Adele said, "all those cases where it's obvious ...."

"Mom, I can tell you any number of cases this year where a guy sitting on death row has been let out because a 'new' piece of evidence came along and showed that somebody else did it. If you look hard, you'll see that the 'new' evidence consists of facts the police and prosecution suppressed. How many of these stories do you think there were so far in Texas this year?"

"Well—"

"There were four. And the year's not over yet."

"But, damn it, when they confess—" Herb said.

"Confess?" Ashley laughed. "Dad, you ought to see what some of these 'confessed criminals' look like after their 'confessions.'"

"Hey, skip the lawyer talk," Herb said. "I bet there are plenty of cases where the guy admits to his lawyer he did it."

"Sure there are, but does that mean he did it? With every big crime there are a dozen nuts who come forward and say they did it, even when they were miles away at the time. I'll give you an actual case. A guy threatens to kill you next time he sees you outside, and you know he carries a pistol all the time. So one night you shoot him in the back, because you figure it's either him or you."

"Hey, that's self-defense."

"Sorry, Dad, it's self-defense only if you believe he's about to kill you right then and there."

"That's crazy. You mean I have to wait until he pulls a gun on me?"

"Right. It's what he does, not what he says. That's the law. So, since you can't plead self-defense, do you want to bargain a plea and take five to ten years in jail, or plead not guilty and make the state prove its case?"

"Hell, I'll plead not guilty."

"Let's say I find a technical loophole in the state's case which will get you off. What would you ask me to do?"

I have to admit I enjoyed watching Herb squirm as he labored for an answer. At that moment he represented to me all the cocky corporate lawyers and captains of industry who look down on us of the criminal bar as if we were something stuck to the bottom of their shoes.

"Well, shit," Herb said, "I guess you have a point. I wouldn't want you to plead me guilty. But what if the guy's guilty and there isn't any way out?"

"I tell him right at the start, 'If you want to plead guilty, that's okay by me. I'll bargain for the lightest sentence I can get. Otherwise, you can tell me as much or little as you want, but if you change your story, I can't put you on the stand to testify, because that would be assisting in perjury.'"

"So what the heck do you do?"

"We sit back and talk about what might have happened and how it came about, just like a detective story. You can always look at a situation several ways: that your client did it, or that somebody else did it, or that some group did it, and it can all be logical or crazy as hell. Sometimes the jury loves an off-the-wall explanation. It's amazing how you can look at the facts and get them to go either way. The beauty of it is that if the jury's confused or in doubt, they won't convict."

76

"Yeah, but when you know—"

"It's not what *I* know, but what the state can prove."

Adele had a troubled look on her face and asked, "But Ashley dear, is that justice?"

"Mother, it is not justice, but it is the law. Only with God is there justice. Quite frankly, the law is a game, and you better make sure you have the best players on your side."

FOUR

All through the *Strafford* trial, I worried about Ashley's physical condition. He seldom slept more than three hours a day. When he concluded a final argument to the jury, his shirt looked as wet as if he had come in from a downpour. The media, however, imposed a greater stress on him than his trials. At every important hearing, reporters surrounded him like jackals gnawing on a lion's kill. I often had to form a flying wedge of our sturdiest associates to break through the pack. Although he appeared alert when the clerk called the *Hear ye,* I feared that his continued sleep deprivation would sap his health and cloud his intellectual vigor.

After the *Strafford* trial, I pressed him to take a vacation. He rebuffed my pleas and swore he would never rest as long as the justice system put innocent men and women on the rack. After a long bout with the flu, he finally agreed to spend a weekend in Palm Desert.

The Monday morning after his return, the newspapers and television channels competed to achieve the greatest shock by their reports and photographs of the axe murders of Olaf and Svea Lothbrook and their daughter, Lucia.

There is something about a murder with a weapon as brutal as an axe that draws public attention on a scale never reached by killings with a pistol, knife, or shotgun. The Lizzie Borden axe murders, for example, still linger in popular memory a century later, while ordinary murders, even those executed by beautiful and wealthy women, lie forgotten in the police archives.

Olaf and Svea Lothbrook and their children, Reginald, age sixteen, and Lucia, age eighteen, lived at the end of a residential street near the city limits of Norwood, a small town in the middle of the rugged Plumas Forest in northern California. They had neighbors on two sides and across the street. On the fourth side Burnt Creek had carved out a steep ravine. The wood siding of their home, like that of their neighbors, was grown over with moss and lichens, giving the street a deserted appearance. A cedar fence ringed their house; in back there was a small shack for storing tools.

At 6:00 A.M. on Sunday, February 13, 1983, Esko and Eylie Raapala, an octogenarian couple immediately to the west of the Lothbrooks, were awakened by the barking of Sassy, Svea Lothbrook's miniature poodle. Esko went to his bedroom window and saw Sassy gyrating around the Lothbrook's front porch, barking and whining so hard she nearly choked. Esko sensed trouble. Sassy was a notorious "yapper," and the Lothbrooks never allowed her outside the house by herself (except for calls of nature) lest she disturb the neighbors.

Esko called the Lothbrooks. There was no answer.

Eylie told him to go next door and make sure everything was all right. He pulled his overalls over his nightshirt, laced up his boots, and crossed the lawn between the two houses.

The front door was wide open. Esko leaned inside and twice shouted, "Everything okay, folks?" When he heard no reply, he stepped inside, but stopped dead when he saw bloody footprints on the stair carpet.

Esko raced out of the house and almost collided with Jed Finsrud, a young neighbor from across the street who had also been awakened by Sassy's barking. Esko rushed back to his house without speaking to Jed and told Eylie to call the police because "things didn't look right" in the Lothbrook house.

Jed Finsrud had more courage or more curiosity than Esko. He edged his way up the stairs beside the bloody footprints. He said later he wished he had stopped, because he would never be able to erase from his mind the scene in Olaf and Svea's bedroom. The floor was awash in blood and seepings from the Lothbrooks' entrails. Olaf and Svea lay on the floor by their beds, hacked to death by blows that Jed guessed had been made by an axe. He raced outside and vomited on the front lawn.

The police photographs of the scene caused me to react the same way. According to the state's forensic pathologist, the assailant attacked Olaf, the father, first. The cause of his death was a powerful blow to the back of his neck. Apparently Olaf had retained enough energy to rise from his bed before slumping to the floor, where he expired. The first blow to Svea, the mother, hit her in the chest. The coroner guessed she had been sitting up in bed, probably awakened by her husband's struggle. The murderer's second blow knocked her to the floor. The third blow, to the heart, was fatal.

The daughter, Lucia, lay on the floor outside her bedroom. The coroner speculated that she had been awakened by the noises in her parents' bedroom and had gone to the hallway to investigate. When she saw the murderer in her path, she ran back towards her room. A blow to her skull killed her at once.

The murderer tried to sever the heads and limbs of the three victims. He must have found it hard work, since he succeeded only in severing the father's head, an arm of the mother, and the two hands of the daughter. The state's forensic pathologist counted a total of forty-seven wounds.

The coroner placed the time of death of all three victims between 5:30 and 5:45 A.M., just fifteen minutes or so before Sassy's barking roused the Raapalas and Finsruds from bed. Jed Finsrud thought that Sassy's barks might have caused the murderer to leave before he had completed his butchery. "The way that dog barks," Jed said, "it's enough to drive off a pack of wolves." The murderer had left a door open, giving Sassy the opportunity to summon help in her canine fashion.

There was no trace of Reginald Lothbrook, Olaf's and Svea's son. Olaf's pickup truck was gone and his double-bitted axe was missing from its hanger on the wall of the tool shack. Sheriff Sigurd Waelsung found its sheath on the ground outside the door. He also found behind the shack a pile of blood-stained clothing, apparently thrown away in haste. It was later identified as Reginald's.

When a search of the town failed to locate Reginald, Sigurd sent out an all-points bulletin for him and the pickup truck. A timber crew spotted the truck on Monday, one day after the murder, on a logging road ten miles outside town. It was hung up on a tree stump in an area that had been clear-cut within the past week. The crew radioed Sigurd and he arrived within minutes. He took the keys from the pickup's ignition and unlocked a tool chest in the truck bed. Inside it he found a double-bitted axe with Olaf's initials burnt into the handle. The blade was caked with blood, tissue, and hair.

A mile down the road, Reginald sat propped against a stump, a serene expression on his face. When Sigurd stepped in front of him, he said, "Hi, Sigurd. What brings you all the way up here?"

"Your family's been murdered."

"Those pigs? Who cares?"

Sigurd read Reginald his rights, handcuffed him, and took him into custody.

The following Tuesday afternoon, Harald Lothbrook, Reginald's uncle, sat in Ashley's office pleading with him to assume Reginald's defense. Before deciding whether to accept, Ashley sent me to visit the town of Norwood and prepare a psychological profile showing the mood of its citizens and the tensions in the community.

Within a week I gave him the following report:

The town of Norwood is set in the middle of the Plumas Forest, about 200 miles northeast of San Francisco. The chief industry of the town is logging. Every day men, women, and machines clear-cut stands of pine, fir, spruce, and hemlock that have stood in solemn majesty on the mountainsides for thousands of years. Where massive trees once shaded the forest floor, there now remain bedraggled hillsides of stumps and weeds.

Within the city limits, however, the old trees have been spared. They line the streets like giant sentinels, reducing even the most grandiose residence to the dimensions of a tar-paper shack.

Norwood residents are nearly all Scandinavians or Finns; nine-tenths of them are fair-complected and tow-headed. I loved to observe the school children in the playground, bobbing like daffodils in the breeze and chattering away in musical Finnish, Norwegian, and Swedish as they played their games.

I interviewed persons at all levels of Norwood society, from Sawyer Holzhauer, the president of Blackriver Lumber Company, down to Len Bailey, the courthouse loafer. None of them could offer any explanation for the killings. They all agreed that Reginald Lothbrook was the "last person" they would expect to inflict bodily harm on anybody, let alone his parents and his sister.

How many times have I heard such "last person" statements made about a man or woman who has perpetrated an unspeakable crime!

Lucia, the daughter, was a high-spirited girl, a senior at the Plumas High School and the Homecoming Queen. Judging by her pictures, she was a great beauty. Reginald utterly lacked his sister's vivacity and warmth, and his unconcealed arrogance made him an outsider to all but a handful of his classmates.

Reginald was a brilliant student. By his sophomore year, when the tragedy occurred, he had exhausted the course offerings at Norwood High. He pled to be admitted to the University of California at Berkeley, but his family and teachers thought he should mature another year or two before moving to the Bay Area.

Reginald's father, Olaf, was the logging supervisor for the Burnt Creek sector of Blackriver Lumber Company and a giant of a man. He carried 250 pounds of solid muscle on a six-and-a-half-foot frame. By one of those odd couplings in which human nature abounds, Olaf's wife, Svea, was a doll-like woman, perfect in every detail of her five feet, two inches and ninety-five pounds.

When I returned to San Francisco and gave Ashley the report of my trip to Norwood, I received the only dressing down of our relationship. "Knute," he said, "I didn't ask for a Baedeker Guide to Norwood. I wanted a motive for the killings, something I could use in Reginald's defense."

I was deeply hurt by his comments. I had labored over

my summary and considered it a model of on-the-scene reporting. Even now, when I have dedicated my life to writing and spent over a hundred hours in composition classes, I am unable to improve upon the language I used then.

Harald Lothbrook was Olaf Lothbrook's older brother. He was a bachelor who had made a considerable fortune importing Scandinavian furniture in the 1950s and 1960s. As a result of Olaf's death, Reginald and Harald were the last direct male descendants of Leif Lothbrook, a hero in the wars of Charles XII. Harald feared that if Reginald were found guilty, the Lothbrook line would die with him. Although Harald had made no personal effort to continue the line, he was willing to spend a substantial part of his fortune to ensure that Reginald would remain at liberty to perpetuate the noble name. The year before the murders he told Olaf he would settle one million dollars on Reginald if he produced a male child, and another million if he named it after the valiant Leif Lothbrook.

Harald offered to pay Ashley any sum he named for Reginald's acquittal. Ashley never told me the amount of the retainer he received, but hinted that it was "quite liberal." His agreement with Harald provided, however, that if Reginald were convicted, or if he were acquitted on the grounds of insanity, Ashley would be compensated only at his standard hourly rate.

Ashley and I visited Reginald in jail two days after his arrest. Although I have found at least one appealing quality in all our murder clients, I found none in Reginald. His eyes were pale blue, almost colorless; his lips were always drawn back in a superior, mocking grin. His first words to us were, "Well, well, look at what Uncle Harald dug up." When we tried to elicit facts we could use in his defense, he said, "That's what you're being paid to do. If you're such hot lawyers, you figure it out." He resented our impositions on his valuable time and treated us like lackeys whose sole function on this earth was to keep him from the gas chamber.

Ashley saw the futility of pointing out to Reginald that we were there to serve his interests. Instead of approaching him with his customary "I'm your friend and protector" appeal, Ashley acted as if he had wandered into Reginald's cell by happenstance and, once there, had decided to stay and profit from Reggie's superior knowledge. Ashley never attempted to lead him into a discussion of the crime or his feelings towards his family. He let Reginald decide the subject of each day's colloquy. The one time Ashley mentioned the family, Reginald said with a snarl, "Don't ever mention those pigs to me again." He manifested no grief over the slayings, and neither denied nor admitted that he was the murderer. He assumed the attitude that their demise was a historical fact and, however it came about, the world was a better place without them.

Reginald despised his teachers, his classmates, the residents of Norwood, in fact, all the inhabitants of the earth, with the exception of Stephen Hawking, the physicist, whom he considered the only human being near his own intellectual level. We never learned of anyone or anything else he liked, except trees.

This was a trial where I felt the best we could hope for was a finding of insanity. But Ashley's uncanny intuition had once more attained an insight denied to me, and he decided against an insanity plea. "If we did that," he said, "he'll stay locked up somewhere, and Uncle Harald will not be satisfied with that outcome." He added with a wink, "We're going for broke on this one. It's all or nothing."

As we left prison, he announced that he was driving that evening to Norwood to gather more background material on Reginald. With his usual tact, he refrained from saying that he was completing the work I had left undone. Graceful touches like this leave me with many happy memories of my years with Ashley.

He showed his faith in my abilities by entrusting me to prepare a motion to exclude from evidence the axe found by Sheriff Waelsung in the toolbox of the Lothbrook pickup. I argued to the court that the axe had been found as a result of a search without a warrant. The prosecution contended that the discovery of the axe was a natural incident of the arrest. Whatever the merits of the arguments on each side, our motion to suppress was, in all honesty, won before we made it, not because of my brief and oral argument, but because Ashley was able to arrange to have the motion heard by the Honorable Jack Reed. Reed was not necessarily a "defendant judge," but at times he found it difficult to bring legal principles into clear focus and, in any but the clearest case, wavered between excluding and admitting evidence and ended up excluding it, not on the basis of precedent, but because he considered it the safer course in the event the case went to the Court of Appeal. As a result, the axe, the one piece of evidence which would almost certainly have sent our client to the gas chamber, never reached the eyes or ears of the jury.

Ashley and I considered whether we should attempt to exclude any statements Reginald made subsequent to his arrest. In the end, we decided not to argue the point for two reasons: one, there were no legal grounds for exclusion, such as duress or failure to give the *Miranda* warning; and, two, the comments Reginald was alleged to have made were not particularly damaging. What Reginald had said to Sheriff Waelsung was much along the line of what he had told us in jail, that his family "was a bunch of pigs" and that "it's up to you cops to find out who did it." Unfortunate words, to be sure, but not by themselves incriminating.

On his return from Norwood, Ashley told the receptionist that he did not wish to be disturbed by anybody. When I failed to reach him at home over the weekend, I assumed he had gone to a hideaway out of town.

He called me Monday morning at six and told me to meet him in his office at once. I settled myself in a comfortable chair and said, "By the look on your face, you've come up with something."

He nodded. "Let me try this out on you. When you

were in Norwood did you sense that there were two warring camps in the town?"

I frowned. "You mean between the loggers and everybody else?"

"Not quite. Between the young and their parents."

"How do you mean?"

He stood up and paced between his desk and a window, hands clasped behind his back. "Clear-cutting, Knute! Didn't you pick up on the conflict over clear-cutting?"

I shook my head. "Clear-cutting? No, not a word."

"It's a very emotional issue. It's the kids against their parents. The town was ready to explode."

"Really?" I said. Somehow, I couldn't picture Norwood as an emotional cauldron.

"Definitely, very definitely, Knute. Violence was inevitable. The town teetered on the brink of a bloodbath. Now that the Lothbrook family has been sacrificed, people hope that peace will return."

I was puzzled. "Who's against clear-cutting?"

Ashley sighed. "The children, every one of the kids is against it. They're outraged. They say their parents are destroying the environment for a quick buck, and there won't be any trees left for them and their children and their grandchildren."

"I never heard anything about that."

"Knute, you have to know how to win the confidence of the young. It takes time. When they see you as a friend, they'll tell you all you want to know. I spent hours listening to them, bought them malts and pizzas, gave them tickets to football games and hard-rock concerts. Once they saw I was their friend, they opened up."

I was still puzzled. "How does any of that relate to our case for Reginald?"

"Don't you see? Reginald was one of them."

"Reginald opposed clear-cutting? But his father was the logging supervisor."

"Precisely. So find out if there are any environmentalists in the jury pool."

"So you're saying he murdered his father, mother, and sister, because of his father's logging? Who's going to believe that? And what was his motivation? It doesn't make any sense."

"Don't you see, Knute? He had to be a hero."

I must admit that, lacking Ashley's antennae, I had never during my long weekend in Norwood received a hint that the town was divided over clear-cutting, nor could I visualize how such a controversy would assist our defense of Reginald.

That afternoon Ashley sent me back to Norwood with a list of the kinds of witnesses he needed and the testimony he expected them to give. Every day for a week I sent him a packet containing the names and photos of potential witnesses and an outline of their testimony. I also hired a photographer to take pictures of the cut areas and the virgin timber stands to provide before-and-after views of the devastation caused by clear-cutting.

Ashley seemed satisfied with my material, but I was no

closer than before to understanding its relevance to our case. The prosecution seemed equally baffled by our witness lists and exhibits. As far as I could tell, they interviewed only two of our witnesses and readily stipulated to the admission of our photographs, subject to challenge at the trial on the grounds of relevance.

Clark Darrow, the prosecutor, did a competent job of putting in the state's case, but he was obviously frustrated by his inability to introduce the blood-stained axe into evidence. Without it, he had to resort to inference—what we lawyers call "circumstantial evidence"—to show that Reginald was the murderer. First, he demonstrated through two experts that the blood-stained clothing left behind the shed belonged to Reginald and that the stains on it were made by the blood of the three victims. Ashley extracted an admission from the state's hematologist that the blood stains could have resulted from Reginald's attempts to minister to the dying, that the blood was of a common type which could have come from other persons, and that it was possible the murderer had taken Reginald's clothing and dipped it in the blood of the victims. Fortunately for us, the trial judge, Jack Muir, was a Creationist who distrusted "scientific" evidence, and sustained our motion to dismiss the state's DNA evidence.

Next, Darrow introduced the evidence of Reginald's flight from the scene of the crime and his unfortunate remarks to Sheriff Waelsing upon his arrest. Ashley countered by trapping the sheriff into an acknowledgment that Reginald's flight could have been caused by emotional upset or by fear for his own life, and that his frequent dismissal of his family as "pigs" proved at most a latent hostility, not premeditated murder.

All in all, however, the prosecution made a strong *prima facie* case, and Judge Muir denied our motion to dismiss.

Our first witness was Kairo Ruti. She was a round, cheerful young woman, and her speech was rapid and musical, like the springtime call of a house finch. It was hard not to smile when she spoke.

Ashley established that she was a classmate of Reginald and led her through the following direct testimony:

Q: Norwood is a logging town, is it not?

A: Yes, sir.

Q: Would you say that logging is its principal activity?

A: Yes, sir.

Q: Are you familiar with most of the people in Norwood?

A: Yes, sir, I know everybody. It's just a hick town.

[laughter]

Q: Are you familiar with their occupations?

A: Yes, sir. Like I said, it's a small town.

Q: Would you say that most of the people in town derive their income from logging?

A: Absolutely. You stop the logging and we're a ghost town. You couldn't sell a pizza if you tried.

Q: Does logging seem important to your parents' generation?

A: You bet. That's all they think about. They worry

that some dope from the EPA will find a spotted owl in the woods around town.

[laughter and a few whistles]

The Court: Spectators are warned that no outbursts will be tolerated from the audience.

Mr Darrow: Your Honor, I fail to see the relevance of this line of questioning.

The Court: I was wondering when you would ask. Gentlemen, will you please approach the bench.

[side bar conference] Mr Blackwood: Judge, the defense contends that my client committed first-degree murder, therefore premeditated—

The Court: I am aware of the law, counsel.

Mr Blackwood:—and I intend to show that if, hypothetically, Mr Lothbrook committed the crime charged, he acted from his passion to protect the trees, not out of premeditation.

Mr Darrow: I don't see what logging has to do with the murder of three innocent people.

The Court: I'll give you a chance to connect it up, Mr. Blackwood, but it had better be good.

Mr Blackwood: Thank you, Your Honor.

Q: [by Mr Blackwood] Now, Miss Ruti, we were talking about logging and its importance to the adult population of Norwood. How do you, as one of the younger residents of Norwood, feel about logging?

A: I hate what it's doing to the town. It's terrible. I step outside the city limits and I think I'm in a cemetery, all those stumps sticking up in the air like tombstones.

Q: Do you find it emotionally upsetting?

A: You betcha! I get cramps every time I hear one of those big trees fall.

Q: Have you talked to other students about clear-cutting?

A: Lots of times.

Q: And how do they feel?

A: Just the same as me, maybe even more so.

Q: But you realize that without the logging, there wouldn't be jobs, don't you?

A: No way. There's lots of jobs around. With a little bit of training, you can get super jobs anywhere. I say, save the trees and build houses out of bricks.

Ashley questioned three other students along the same line, and they all testified that they were upset and angry about the clear-cutting. Sandy Cray, one of Reginald's classmates, said it was strange that parents insisted on their children's learning the latest computer programs, when the parents, for their part, refused to train themselves for more profitable careers. "They're a bunch of hypocrites," he said, "and lazy to boot." Other youthful witnesses expressed the feeling that the greed and sloth of the older generation were depriving them of their inheritance and leaving them a country despoiled and polluted.

Ashley introduced photographs of the clear-cut areas and contrasted them with pictures of virgin timber. The objections of the prosecutor were, to my surprise, overruled by Judge Muir. I suspected he was a Preservationist as well as a Creationist.

At the close of the second day of direct testimony by the defense, I sensed the direction Ashley was taking. He recalled Kairo Ruti to the stand and questioned her as follows:

Q: You testified before, Miss Ruti, that you knew most of the people in town and their occupations, did you not?

A: Yes, sir.

Q: Did you know the occupation of the late Olaf Lothbrook?

A: Sure. He was in charge of logging for Blackriver.

Q: Blackriver Lumber Company?

A: Right.

Q: So was he the one who decided which areas to cut and how to cut them?

Mr Darrow: I object your Honor, lack of foundation.

By the Court: Sustained.

Q: [By Mr Blackwood]: Did you ever attend a debate at which Mr Lothbrook talked about clear-cutting?

A: Yes, at the high school.

Q: And did he tell the audience that he was in charge of logging for the Blackriver Lumber Company and that he decided which trees to cut and how?

A: Yes, sir, he did. He said he told the crews where to cut and how to go about it. He said clear-cutting was the quickest and safest way to harvest the timber.

Q: So from what he said, you understood he was responsible for all the clear-cutting in the Norwood area.

A: Yes, sir.

Q: Did you know that Reginald Lothbrook, the defendant, was his son?

A: Yes.

Q: Was Reginald popular with his classmates before February 13, the date of the murders?

A: No way. We all knew his dad was in charge of the clear-cutting. We avoided him.

Ashley then entered into a dangerous but crucial line of questioning.

Q: Now after the defendant was indicted, did you have occasion to talk to your classmates about him in connection with the murders?

A: Sure.

Q: What did they say about him then?

A: We all thought he was a hero.

Q: A hero? From being an "outsider" he became a "hero?"

A: You got it.

Q: Is it fair to say that you considered him a hero on the assumption that he was the one who committed the murders of Olaf Lothbrook and his wife and daughter?

Mr Darrow: Objection. Counsel is leading the witness.

The Court: Overruled. The witness may answer.

A: Sure. It was a super thing to do. Of course, we felt bad about Lucia. She was a swell kid, and everybody liked Svea. But here Reginald—anyway, we assumed it was Reginald—went out and sacrificed himself and his family to save our forests. We all felt he was a hero.

At this point the prosecution must have believed that Ashley had handed it the case.

Ashley continued:

Q: But you had no way of knowing that the defendant

had in fact committed the crime, right? None of you were present, and none of you had any knowledge other than what you read or heard—correct?

A: Sure, but—

Q: It was your assumption from what you heard and read and, on the basis of that assumption, the defendant went from being an outsider to being a hero. Is that correct?

A: Right. We felt he was our avenger, an avenging angel.

Q: An avenging angel?

A: Right. He wanted to save our forests. No one else did anything. They just talked. He gave his life and family for us.

The theory of Ashley's defense was at last clear to me and, no doubt, to the prosecution.

Ashley followed up Kairo's testimony by establishing through several more witnesses Reginald's sudden elevation from "outsider" to "angel of the forests." Now I understood why Ashley had insisted on impaneling all the environmentalists in the jury pool. I waited eagerly to hear his closing argument.

Although not a landmark of legal advocacy like his "*tabula rasa*" speech in the *Tyler* case, it is well worth the attention of anyone interested in forensic oratory.

"Ladies and gentlemen of the jury," he said, "you know that emotional issues are capable of producing great crimes, crimes which would not otherwise have occurred. So let us step back for a moment from the emotions of this case—and a very emotional case it is. Let us take a moment to recall the pictures you saw of our virgin forest lands laid waste, of ancient stands of pine, spruce, and fir that have stood in solemn majesty since the founding of this nation, mercilessly razed, the grandfathers and great-grandfathers of the forest sliced and minced into sawdust and boards to build new houses in Japan and Germany. Consider that we will never, neither we, nor our children, nor our grandchildren, nor our great-grandchildren, see these giants of the forest again.

"Much as this pillage of our national heritage distresses us—pillage which enriches only a wealthy few—much as this devastation sickens our souls, think how much more it pains the children of Norwood, who have to live in the middle of this carnage and watch, hour by hour, day after day, the forests they love fall to the axe and the saw. Are you surprised that one of these children might have felt the need to stop this sacrilege? Do you wonder at the fact that some young person made it his or her cause to intercede on behalf of Nature, no matter what his personal loss might be, so that future generations could possess in perpetuity what we now enjoy? In Norwood alone there must be fifty young men and women who would commit such a crime in order to spare the forests. Any one of them could have carried out these killings and made it look as if it had been done by the defendant.

"Such heroism need not surprise us. Countless times in our history, ever since the days of our Pilgrim Fathers, men and women have sacrificed their ease and prosperity, even their lives, so that future generations might live as well as they lived, so that the blessings they enjoyed might also be enjoyed by their children and grandchildren.

"Do we call people who make these sacrifices criminals? No, we honor them. We erect bronze tablets in their honor at forest entrances. We name woodlands and mountains and parks after them.

"And what do the young men and women of Norwood call such a person? An angel, an 'angel of the forest.' And they are right. The young see the world more clearly than we. Our consciences have been dulled by years of compromise, but the young believe that someone who risks his life to protect our pristine forests deserves praise, not punishment. And so say I. And that is what I ask you to say to this court, this state, and to the world."

When Ashley sat down, I whispered to him that after hearing his speech, the jury would certainly have to vote for an acquittal. "No, Knute," he said, "when there are three dead bodies and the defendant didn't take the stand, a deadlock's the best we can hope for."

And so it was. The jury stayed deadlocked for eight days before the court declared a mistrial. The result raised an interesting question for Ashley. As I mentioned, Ashley's retainer agreement with Uncle Harald provided for him to be compensated on a straight hourly basis, but if he obtained an acquittal, he would receive a sizeable bonus. The agreement failed to specify what his compensation would be in the event of an acquittal resulting from a mistrial. Ashley argued that he was entitled to the bonus, since the mistrial disposed of the immediate litigation as fully as an outright acquittal. I never learned how he and Uncle Harald resolved their differences. Since Harald hired another attorney to handle the retrial, I expect that he and Ashley parted on less than a cordial footing.

On retrial Reginald was convicted of first-degree murder on three counts and sentenced to the gas chamber. Reading the newspaper article reminded me that Ashley had never enunciated a Rule in Reginald's case. I asked him what it should be.

He laughed. "I don't think I thought of it at the time, Knute, but it came to me later: *IDENTIFY YOUR DEFENDANT WITH A POPULAR CAUSE AND PICK YOUR JURY ACCORDINGLY.*"

"Very good," I said. "Now let me ask you another question. How would you have handled Reginald's retrial?"

Ashley stroked his chin a moment. "Frankly, Knute, the second time around I would have pleaded insanity."

"You mean—"

"We were damn lucky. We shot for the moon and managed to knock a piece off it. We wouldn't have been that lucky a second time. You're allowed only one miracle a lifetime."

FIVE

After the conclusion of the *Lothbrook* trial in 1983, Ashley again toyed with the idea of devoting himself to civil practice, but dismissed it after a week, saying that it never stimulated him to exert his best efforts, and once more his health crumbled under the stress of criminal practice. He neglected his exercise schedule and draped himself in double-breasted suits to conceal his expanded frame. A climb up a staircase in the courthouse left him out of breath.

Since his parents' visit in 1982, he had never been away from the office for more than three days in a row. When at home, he spent all his time reading transcripts and court reports. I urged him to take a vacation, this time for at least a month. He said he was too busy. To placate me, he promised to go on a diet and resume regular sessions with his personal trainer. Within a few weeks, I noticed a marked improvement in his appearance.

On June 4, 1984, an event took place which made my concerns about his health seem trivial and rattled even Ashley's *sang-froid*.

As we walked down the steps of the Hall of Justice,

I heard the sound of a shot fired at close range and the whine of a bullet ricocheting near my head. I pulled Ashley down to the ground, filthy as it was. When my heart resumed something like a regular beat, I looked up and saw dozens of police swarming around and over the courthouse steps like fire ants whose nest has been disturbed by a hapless picnicker. I was relieved that no one appeared to have been injured.

"Good God!" I said to Ashley. "Do you think someone was trying to kill us?"

He shook his head. "Not a chance."

I rose to my feet and looked over the shoulder of an officer who was studying a chip in the gray stone facade inches away from where our heads had been a minute ago. He turned to Ashley and me and said, "You guys were standing here when the shot was fired, right?" We nodded. "So, you know some guy wants you dead?"

"No, officer," Ashley said with a smile, "I'm sure it was just another California drive-by shooting. I'm a defense attorney. The only people gunning for me are the police, and they don't miss."

The officer scowled. Police on duty seldom exhibit a sense of humor.

Despite the smile on Ashley's face, I knew he must have been as shaken as I, and I asked myself whether he might be trying to ignore some danger that threatened both of us. I suggested that we stop at a delicatessen nearby before returning to the office and have a cup of coffee and a croissant to quiet our nerves. He agreed, and I made use of the opportunity to renew my suggestion that he take a full month's vacation. This time he agreed that he needed a long rest. "Knute, I'll take August off and start a project I've had in mind for several years."

I asked him the nature of his project. "I'll tell you, but you must promise to keep it a secret," he said. I assured him I would. "I'm going to write my memoirs. I'll pitch the book to non-lawyers. Laymen want to understand how criminal lawyers work, but ninety percent of the guys who write courtroom best-sellers don't know the first thing about winning a *real* criminal case. They're just writing for the money. I want the people of America to see what really goes on in their courtrooms."

"Ashley," I said, "it's the book the country's been waiting for! Tell me how I can help you."

Ashley was encouraged by my enthusiasm and said he would start working on his book during his month off. I offered him the use of the little cabin Mamie and I had built up in the Sierras. Ashley was touched by my offer, but said he wanted to see Europe. His secretary, Maxine Gregg, had found a tour where in four weeks he could visit two or three cities in every country of Western Europe, from Oslo to Athens, from Dublin to Budapest.

After his death, I searched his files and found no evidence that he had ever started on his memoirs. I surmised that, once he seated himself at the keyboard and started typing, he came face-to-face with the writer's struggle to translate thoughts to words and arrange them so that they come to life. Ideas clear as crystal in concept, cloud and darken as they move to the printed page; phrases that seem to illuminate an experience have, on rereading, all the impact of a Treasury regulation.

My sons, Brutus and Alexander, were great favorites of Ashley's. All the love he might have lavished on his own children, nieces, and nephews, he expended on my boys. Each Christmas and birthday, his presents were the most expensive ones they received. One year would bring an electric train, another year a chemistry set, portable radio, or miniature electric car. As soon as a new toy came on the market, Ashley found some pretext to buy it for the boys. (I suspect those rascals of mine gave him some pretty specific hints about what they wanted.) He planned many excursions with them to the circus, the movies, or some other amusement, but when the day arrived, he inevitably found that his time had been preempted by an office emergency and ended up handing me the tickets and the opportunity to share in my boys' youthful merriment. I often felt that Ashley would have been a happier man if he had chosen the pleasures of wife, children, and the other comforts of settled domesticity, but he elected to dedicate his life to the law. He told me that a man could not pursue the cause of justice without depriving his wife and children of the love and guidance they deserved.

His absence gave me an opportunity to carry out a project which had occupied my attention ever since reading the letter he received from his former fiancée, Amy Bontemps. What was there about A&A Social Services that had caused her to refer to it in such opprobrious terms? Was it possible that Ashley had failed to tell me the whole truth? During our four years together, I had never seen him distort or conceal the truth from me in any way. Still, my legal training taught me not to trust the spoken word unless corroborated by independent facts. Impelled by the need to know the truth, I proposed to Mamie that, while Ashley was in Europe, we take time off to visit our numerous relatives on the Iron Range. Every summer our parents begged us to visit them and bring the boys to play with their Minnesota cousins. I put them off repeatedly because of business pressures and instead sent them airline tickets to visit us in California. Neither Mamie nor I have any enthusiasm for large family gatherings on the Range, since—not to put too fine a point upon it—they tend to end in drunken orgies accompanied by fisticuffs.

My plan was to spend only two evenings in Eveleth and the rest of my time in Minneapolis learning what I could about A&A Social Services. It took me nearly ten days of exhaustive effort, but I have never regretted the time spent. It confirmed my belief in Ashley's integrity and provided me all the facts I needed to expose the lies of some feminists who have sacrificed their childbearing years to search for materials with which to blacken Ashley's reputation.

During his junior year in high school, Ashley became engaged to a classmate, Amy Bontemps. Even then Ashley knew that he would follow the law and started taking the steps to ensure that his grades would entitle him to a full scholarship to Stanford. He also realized that he would need substantial amounts of cash for their home, furniture, cars, and entertainment. After considering several business options, he and Amy initiated a dating service by the name of "A&A Social Services." It was a happy union of an entrepreneurial spirit with a social service. Ashley's enemies have, as usual, distorted the nature of their business, but I have researched every available reference to A&A and interviewed the participants, and I can say categorically that I have in my possession all the relevant facts about A&A Social Services.

The company was founded on the premise that many adolescent boys and girls are eager to form relationships with persons of the opposite sex, but are often too bashful to make a contact or too unsophisticated to succeed. The service charged an annual membership fee plus a service fee for each date it arranged for its members. Ashley enrolled the boys and Amy recruited the girls. They had the enrollees speak for two minutes on tape so that subscribers could judge their personal and intellectual attributes. For an additional fee, A&A suggested an entertainment both might enjoy, bought the tickets, made the reservations, and prepared a list of topics of mutual interest. If the couple preferred to spend the evening by themselves, the service put a private facility at their disposal.

By their senior year, Ashley and Amy were servicing students from high schools throughout Minneapolis and its suburbs. In six months A&A became the most successful enterprise ever launched by high school students in the state of Minnesota. In recognition of their achievements, the Jaycees awarded Ashley and Amy a Citation for Distinguished Enterprise at a downtown banquet. Ashley gave a speech praising the capitalist system, and Amy congratulated the Jaycees for their support of the youth of Minneapolis. The governor of Minnesota named them Junior Citizens of the Year and presented them hand-lettered citations and silver medals. A month before graduation they listed the business for sale and made a profit in the high five figures.

Notwithstanding its success and official recognition, Ashley's critics claim that A&A was not what it professed to be and charge that its participants engaged in highly inappropriate conduct. Such allegations are clearly libelous and lack any factual foundation whatsoever. Amy Bontemps is the only participant in A&A who ever came forward with such charges, and her accusations must be viewed as those of a woman scorned. It is obvious that neither the Jaycees nor the governor's office would have honored Ashley and Amy's achievements without a thorough scrutiny of A&A's operation. What's more, Ashley and Amy were engaged and planned to be married during the summer following their high school graduation. It is unthinkable—except to his lifelong foes—that Ashley would have permitted his fiancée to participate in a venture carrying the least taint of impropriety.

I concluded my investigations on A&A over the Labor Day weekend and hastened back to San Francisco to be on hand for the firm's first Thursday evening gathering since Ashley's return from Europe. On this occasion he dispensed with any discussion of business and showed us all the slides and videotapes he had taken during his trip and accompanied them with his oral commentary. In each city he visited he had shot at least one roll of film and one full videotape. It was an inspiring presentation and made us all yearn to travel abroad. When the evening ended, we were amazed to find that it was almost 3 A.M. Ashley was chagrined at having kept us up so late, and told us not to come to the office before ten the next morning unless we had early court appearances. Many of us did, but we laughed and said we weren't tired and, in fact, felt invigorated by the experience of accompanying him on his travels.

During my vacation in Minnesota, I had continued to worry about Ashley's safety, not only for his sake, but also, frankly, for my own. It was hard for me, after four years of association with Ashley, to imagine practicing law with any other attorney. More than one law firm, some of them the most prominent in San Francisco, offered me full partnerships on terms they considered lavish, but at remuneration levels far below those I earned as Ashley's associate. Such was the generosity of the man that not even 400-lawyer firms could match the compensation he paid his associates. So much for those who charge him with greed! Some San Francisco lawyers who should know better, claim that our compensation levels forced us to overcharge our clients. There were, to be sure, cases where we charged more than customary, but only in situations where the outcome justified a premium. A defendant who escapes the gas chamber solely as a result of the skills of Blackwood & Associates and our 72-hour work weeks, rarely questions the cost.

Not that I claim that any of us (except for Ashley) was the most brilliant lawyer in California. However, I'm certain we were the best trained and most highly motivated. A new associate's three-year training period was referred to as the "Inferno." The demands compared to those of a medical resident. From each associate we expected twelve billable hours every day, except for Sundays and national holidays.

Our internal review process placed even greater demands on the body and soul of a First-Degree Associate. Every piece of work, every statement, deposition, motion paper, and client interview he or she produced was studied by a Second-Degree Associate and criticized mercilessly, some might say sadistically. Those who survived the "Inferno"—as only one in four did, and those the pick of their law school class to begin with—became Second-Degree Associates, the equals of any litigator (except Ashley) in the state. A few went on to Third-Degree Associateships. I was the only one to rise to a Fourth-Degree Associateship.

To return to the subject of Ashley's safety, I recognized that Ashley was unlikely to embrace any measures to protect himself. At Mamie's prompting, I called Sergeant Kesselring, a detective on the San Francisco police force who owed me a favor for overturning his dismissal from the force for allegedly raping a teenager held in custody. I told him about the shot fired at us outside the courthouse and asked him to conduct a private investigation and determine whether the shooting was random or intentional, and who the perpetrator might be.

Sergeant Kesselring called back the same day and said the bullet had been located. It had been fired from a .32 caliber handgun. A policeman who had been directing traffic near the courthouse said that after the shot rang out, a woman with blond hair ran to a car and drove away. He hadn't seen a weapon in her hand, but she could easily have concealed a pistol in the large purse she carried.

"It was probably a small pistol, and that's why the shot missed," Kesselring said. "Unless you've had a lot of training, it's hard to hit anything with those toys."

"A woman?" I asked. "How old?"

"Mid-thirties."

"Anything else?"

"She drove off in a rusty Ford sedan with out-of-state plates. He didn't get the state or number, but said there was a big bumper sticker with something on it about mosquitoes."

"Mosquitoes? Anything else?"

"A broad who takes a shot with an un-silenced weapon at a guy in broad daylight outside a courthouse has got to be an amateur. Good news, she's a lousy shot. Bad news, she'll try again, unless she did it just for a one-time thrill. Knute, old buddy, you better buy some life insurance for your friend and yourself. You don't know for sure who she was gunning for."

His words stabbed me like a blade of ice. Who, I wondered, could possibly wish to kill Ashley or me? Our most virulent enemies, more vicious by far than the police, were the local reporters, columnists, and editors, but they attacked with the spoken or the printed word, not firearms. Far from wishing to eliminate us, they depended on us as subjects for their invective. Without us to berate, they would be compelled to hunt down fresh prey for their poisoned shafts. Their relationship to Ashley and me was that of a parasite to its host: when the host dies, the parasite perishes as well.

A day after Sergeant Kesselring and I spoke, something he had said about a mosquito bumper sticker twitched my subconscious. Minnesotans obsess about mosquitoes, and I wondered whether it could have been a Minnesota car. I called Sergeant Kesselring and asked whether his informant remembered if the bumper sticker said something about the mosquito being the state bird.

"Right, I remember him saying something like that. Christ, people up there must be crazy."

"They are."

As I listened to Mamie's snores that night, I remembered the threatening letter Ashley had received two years ago. Hadn't it been written by a woman and postmarked in Minnesota? Could she be the same blonde the officer had seen? I wanted to ask Ashley, but feared that if I raised questions about the shooting, he would brood on my purpose in asking and resurrect the demons he had dismissed during his European vacation. Yet the issue had to be dealt with. Even if Ashley chose to ignore threats to his life, I couldn't in fairness to my family ignore the possibility that what endangered him also endangered me.

The next day, without telling Mamie, I bought an insurance policy on my life and a much larger one on Ashley, but the monetary security they provided could never compensate me for the loss of Ashley's friendship or begin to replace the income I received from Blackwood & Associates.

Ashley and I spent a week in Ukiah, a small town in the Coastal Range, trying the case of Tanya Dzerzhinsky. She was a tall and attractive ballet dancer who engaged in terroristic acts against federal installations during the off-season. She came from Kiev and had carried on similar activities in the U.S.S.R. Once she obtained asylum in the United States, she promptly resumed her old habits. At the trial, she told a story of such suffering under the Communist regime that the jury didn't have the heart to add to her sorrows, just for blowing up a courthouse and killing an attorney.

One evening over dinner at a Tex-Mex restaurant in Ukiah, I said to Ashley, "I have to tell you there seems to be a strong connection between the person who fired that shot at us and the letter you read to me in 1982."

"What letter?"

I smiled. "Ashley, you don't fool old Knute. You know what I mean: the letter from that girl you knew in high school."

"Amy? What makes you think there's a connection?"

I told him what Sergeant Kesselring had said about the bumper sticker. "I just put two and two together. Now tell me if I'm right."

Ashley shoved his dinner plate to the side of the table.

"I better fill you in, Knute. She called me."

"Amy called you? When?"

"A day or two after she got my letter."

"What did she say?"

"I wish I'd taken your advice, Knute, and never responded to her. She was completely unreasonable. She wanted millions from me, or else."

"She threatened your life?" I gasped.

"Definitely. She didn't say what she'd do, but she was wound up so tight she could do anything."

"So, what do we do now?"

"We forget about it and go on trying cases. She's back in Minnesota and we're out here."

"She could drive out again."

"Knute, you don't have any proof she's the one who fired the shot. All you have to go on is the bumper sticker. When you have some hard evidence, I'll take action. So, can we get back to Tanya's case?"

On our return to San Francisco, I suggested to Ashley that we quit criminal law and engage in the quiet routine of personal injury and malpractice work, as we had discussed several times before.

Ashley looked at me as if I had suggested plastering the ceiling of the Sistine Chapel with Coca-Cola ads. "Knute, criminal cases are my life, my art. They are the ultimate challenge of the law. Our clients face the alternatives of life or death. It's the only game that employs all my abilities. Would you ask a Rembrandt to give up painting and sell hamburgers?"

"You're under a lot of stress. How about taking up a hobby? For me, woodworking takes away the tensions of the courtroom, plus it has a practical side. I saved several thousand dollars by making all the furniture for our cabin in the mountains."

"Knute, when would I have time for a hobby? It's all I can do keep up with the new cases and laws. I barely have time for my charitable work and social engagements, not to mention managing the law office. Speaking of which, our lease is coming up for renewal, and we have to think whether we want to buy or sign another five-year lease."

Blackwood & Associates employed at this time twenty lawyers, thirty legal assistants, and some fifty investigators, secretaries, process servers, bookkeepers, gofers, and other staff on two floors of the Thurn & Taxis Tower. The constant inflation of California real property values increased our rents at least twenty percent every time our lease came up for renewal. Ashley decided to build his own office space and stop giving a landlord the benefit of rising property values.

During periods of enforced idleness in the courtroom, he drew sketches for his building. When he arrived at a satisfactory design, he interviewed several architects to see who was most fitted to carry out his intentions. The one he selected was Michelangelo ("Mike") Brunelli, a dark, stocky man with a brush haircut. Mike had never designed an office building; Ashley chose him because he was the only architect who showed any enthusiasm for his design.

"What you got here, Mr Blackwood," Mike said, "is a beautiful Georgian facade. There ain't another one like it in all of northern California. Which brings up a little problem. The city fathers in San Francisco will say the design don't conform, which means it don't look like anything else on the street, that it's, well, not harmonious."

"They can say that?" Ashley asked.

"Yup, and they can make it stick. Of course, up against a lawyer like you, they'd lose, but you don't want to spend three years litigating something without getting a cent for your time, and meanwhile property values are going through the roof. Maybe you should consider building outside San Francisco."

"Like where?"

Mike rubbed his brush cut. "I think I can sell your plans in Oakland. I got some friends over there. I expect they might see the light if you went over and talked to them, you know, take them out for dinner, find out what kinds of problems they're having, be their friend."

Ashley saw that Mike's approach made sense and reluctantly agreed to move our offices across the Bay. Within eighteen months and despite fierce opposition from the neighborhood, Blackwood & Associates was installed in a three-story Georgian building housing some one hundred employees, with the capability of expanding to accom-modate an additional one hundred. The exterior of the building was Boston-type brick; the windows were double-hung, white, and mullioned. All the lawyers' of-fices, except Ashley's, had the same size and furnishings because Ashley did not want his associates arguing about who got what office. "I pay them plenty," he said. "They'll have fewer distractions in a small office. If they're meet-ing a client, they can use a conference room."

The lawyers' offices and the conference rooms were panelled in dark walnut veneer. The chairs were dark oak upholstered with red Naugahyde. Ashley's office and the two reception areas had working gas fireplaces and chair coverings of real leather. The only pictures Ashley allowed on the walls were reproductions of 18th century English prints of hunting scenes and square-rigged sailing ships. Since there were no inexpensive restaurants in the immediate area, Ashley installed a cafe-teria in the basement and had it attended between 7 A.M. and midnight by two cooks, a busboy, and a dishwasher. The food was excellent and the prices were half those one might expect to pay for comparable meals in a restaurant. After midnight, cold snacks, soft drinks, and coffee were available from vending machines. A side benefit was that no time was lost from work beating a path to and from a restaurant on Oakland's clogged streets. Best of all, there was a parking garage under the building which was available to clients *gratis* and to em-ployees for a small monthly rental.

A week after we moved in, Ashley held an open house

for prosecutors, judges, and members of the Bar who had referred cases to him. Every one of the guests, as they partook of California's finest wines and foods, expressed their envy of the superb facilities and tasteful decor.

Ashley confided to me that the cost of the building had far exceeded Mike Brunelli's estimates. "I should have hired an architect with more experience," he said, "but the others wanted to build the same old glass and steel cubes. Mike gave me what I wanted. I'm damned lucky I got that retainer from Gil Derais before the last construction payment came due."

The *Gil Derais* case was not one of Ashley's triumphs, and he was frank to say that he would have turned down the client but for the fact he needed cash for his building.

Gil was accused of assaulting eight female students at colleges in the Bay Area, but no one would have guessed to look at him that he was a serial rapist. He was short, chubby, round-faced, fifty-two, and wore glasses with thin wire rims. He practiced dentistry full-time, even though a recent inheritance of timberland permitted him to retire in comfort, if he so chose. Ordinarily his voice was so low and soft that it was difficult to understand what he said. He had the largest fund of sexist jokes of any man I've ever known, except for Father Jerome, our parish priest, and he told them in a voice so loud Ashley had me shut the door to avoid distracting the staff.

Gil's *modus operandi,* according to the state, was to stop his car at night and inquire of a young woman the way to a college building. Pretending to be befuddled by her instructions, he stepped out and asked her to draw the route on a map he carried. While she marked the map on the hood of the car, he seized her from behind, anesthetized her with chloroform, pushed her into the car, took her to a deserted spot, and tied, gagged, and blindfolded her. When she recovered consciousness, he raped her.

The prosecuting attorney was Ginger Steinem. In Ashley's opinion, she was the best in the state. She had a pleasant voice, a ready smile, and, though slightly plump, a good figure. She would have made an excellent comedienne in the style of Doris Day if she had turned to film, but in the courtroom she was all business. She had perfect control over her features. Opposing counsel could never tell whether a question she asked of a hostile witness was a routine query or the first step in a line of questions which would lead the witness on a path over the edge of a cliff.

Ashley had never encountered Ginger in his previous trials and seemed much taken with her. He dressed with special care when appearing in court and made a point of asking her whether she had had a good weekend, whether her son was over his chicken pox (she was a single parent), and whether her mother and father had enjoyed their stay in town. I hoped that they might form a relationship which would lead to marriage, since his "engagement" to Alexia seemed destined to remain just that. But Ginger never encouraged Ashley to penetrate beyond the superficies of professional collegiality.

Ginger, I am sure, expected that Ashley would in this case, as in his past rape cases, attempt to introduce into evidence the prior sexual history of the alleged victims in order to raise the issue of implied consent. Before the trial Ginger successfully moved Judge Taney to exclude any such evidence on the basis that Gil's method of operation made the issue of "implied consent" irrelevant: a woman who was a stranger to Gil and whom he chloroformed, bound, and gagged, she said, could not, under any circumstances, be considered to have consented. Ashley, however, turned her logic to his own advantage. He agreed that a woman blindfolded and distraught was incapable of giving consent, but argued that by the same token she would be incapable of identifying the perpetrator beyond a reasonable doubt. He utilized another weakness in the state's case, that several of the victims failed to report the rape until weeks later. Two days before trial Gil pled guilty to greatly reduced charges. After a year in prison, he was a free man.

Gil was delighted to have gotten off so lightly and paid us a substantial fee. Bea Benedict, a leading feminist, expressed her rage at the brevity of Gil's sentence. In her weekly newspaper, *Medea,* she wrote:

> "After being punished with a term in prison no longer than a teacher's sabbatical, Gil Derais will be at liberty to once more brutalize the women of California. Let us long remember the unholy compact entered into among Judge Taney, District Attorney Steinem, and that infamous perverter of criminal justice, Ashley Blackwood. Derais's sentence is a mockery of justice. The safety of every woman in the state is in jeopardy."

She ended by calling upon the California Bar Association to commence proceedings to disbar all four of us.

I read the article aloud in the judge's chambers to Ashley, the judge, and Ginger. We had a good laugh over it.

After the *Gil Derais* case, Ashley surprised me by saying over coffee and croissants, "Knute, this time we're really going to do it. No more criminal cases! I'm tired out, and we have big mortgage payments to meet. Now's the time to start building up our estates."

Ashley had made the same promise after the *Strafford* case, only to change his mind when the *Lothbrook* axe murder case came to his desk. I must have looked at him with raised eyebrows because he added, "I've made up my mind, and this time I mean it. No more criminal cases for us for five years! Let the Second and Third-Degree Associates handle them. We'll help some people who really need it and make some money along the way."

And so, until the *Ramona Krafft* case three years later, Ashley and I handled only personal injury and malpractice claims while lower-level associates handled the criminal calendar. Still, Ashley couldn't resist caring for the needs of the poor and the persecuted. Indeed, he led the California Criminal Bar in championing their rights, a part of his life's work that his detractors have chosen to ignore. He told me on more than one occasion that it was an unusual year when he failed to donate at least $100,000 of his time to eleemosynary works. "I'd be a rich man," he said, "if I hadn't been beggared by my charity cases."

In this respect he inherited his mother's, rather than his father's, genes. While I was in Minneapolis researching the history of A&A Social Services, I spent most of a week with Herb and Adele for background information on the book I knew I would some day write about Ashley.

Adele taught American History in high school and worked two evenings a week at a branch library. She whispered to me that her sympathies, like Ashley's, were with the working man and woman. At heart, she was a socialist. She had never disclosed her liberal views to Herb, and I had to promise her to keep them in the strictest confidence.

Herb's political orientation was at the opposite end of the scale from Adele and Ashley's. He championed conservative causes which Ronald Reagan would have dismissed as utopian. He favored a flat tax of fifteen percent on all income other than capital gains, the abolition of all welfare payments, and the direct linkage of Social Security benefits to each individual's contributions to the trust fund. In the long run, he said, the income tax should be replaced with a national sales tax, and the rate of tax should be adjusted up or down to cover budget deficits so that taxpayers would immediately feel the impact of any new government spending programs.

Herb drove buses for the Minneapolis transit system. I asked him how he, a bus driver, came to hold his conservative views. "Before I got my job," he said, "I used to be a bleeding-heart liberal, but a year behind the wheel changed me for good. Travel my route with me. When you see what I've seen, you'll wise up."

I accepted his invitation, and the next day rode with him from 7:00 A.M. until noon. He made sure I paid full fare each way. I placed myself on the other side of the metal partition behind his seat, put a yellow legal pad on my knee, and noted his observations on each passenger. He may have attempted to speak softly, but his voice set up vibrations in my feet like the pedal point of a cathedral organ.

As a young black woman with two small daughters stepped on board, he turned to me and said, hand over his mouth, "This one got knocked up at fifteen, and she's been living on welfare ever since. Never held a job in her life. She's shacked up with a guy twenty years older'n her. He's waiting around until her kids get old enough to knock up. That's where your tax money goes."

He made similarly disparaging remarks about each passenger as he or she boarded, sparing only two attractive young women who called him "Herbie-O." A long-haired man in his forties wearing a worn leather jacket and tattered jeans took violent offense when Herbert characterized him as a "creep who blew his brains out on heroin in 'Nam and is living on a vet's pension paid for by yours truly." The man grasped the steering wheel and threatened to cut out Herb's liver. Herb stopped the bus, opened the door, picked the man up by the collar of his jacket and the seat of his pants, and threw him out on the street, accompanying his actions with a freshet of abuse laden with the imagery of the outhouse.

From some remarks he made during our bus ride,

I gathered that Herb worked evenings and weekends as a bouncer at a bar near his home. The income from his and Adele's part-time jobs, plus the gifts I'm sure Ashley made to them, provided them the means to buy a cabin at Lake Kakabeetowatachee in northern Minnesota. "It's a sanctuary from the cares of the world," he said. "It's where we go to get away from it all. That's real living up there. We're in the middle of the North Woods. The walleyes can't wait to be caught." Even though his cabin had gas, electricity, running water, and satellite television, he described the ambiance as "rustic."

But to return to Ashley's work with the poor, in 1986 he founded a boys' club for disadvantaged youth in Bayview, served on its board, and provided a significant part of its operating capital. Every Monday evening he went to the "clubhouse" and gave the youths free legal advice. These evenings, he said, often lasted until early morning as packs of young men shuffled in and begged Ashley to defend them against charges of drug possession, robbery, and rape. During the initial interview, he discovered that many of his defendants had, in the course of their arrests, been exposed to shocking levels of police brutality. At his own expense he hired a photographer to document their cuts and bruises and used the pictures to support damage suits against the city. At first, not one client in a hundred had the courage to assert his claims of abuse, but six months later, emboldened by a group they had formed with the acronym *PWBV (Prosecutors Will Be Violated)*, every defendant sued as a matter of course. As the level of uniformed brutality rose, the claims filed by Ashley also rose, and the city found itself paying millions in damages to injured plaintiffs, most of whom, by an irony which escaped few at City Hall, received their checks while in jail.

Ashley gave generously of his time to workingmen and women who were victims of age discrimination and could not afford the fees charged by the moguls of the San Francisco Bar. "Once people reach forty-nine,"Ashley said, "employers figure their medical insurance will hit the roof, so they fake an incident of drinking on the job or snorting coke and fire them."

For every terminated employee who retained us because of his or her alleged incompetence or substance abuse, we automatically filed charges of age, sex, or racial discrimination, whichever seemed most appropriate to the occasion, and forced the employer to reinstate our client in his or her job for the months or years it took until some tribunal reached a decision on the employee's competence or sobriety, or until the employer agreed to our settlement terms. These services Ashley performed at no cost to the employee other than the fraction of the wages and awards assigned to Blackwood & Associates.

Because of his success in sex discrimination cases, Ashley was recognized in 1987 as "the champion of the Bay Area workingwoman" and frequently appeared as the keynote speaker at meetings of feminist organizations. At a luncheon of the Gloriana Club he struck up a friendship with Bea Benedict, its president and founder, the same woman who had vilified him in *Medea* during the *Gil*

Derais trial. Although Bea had deplored Ashley's tactics in that case, she recognized his forensic ability. When Ramona Krafft was indicted on charges of mayhem, Bea tapped the resources of several women's groups and managed to lure Ashley back into criminal practice before the expiration of the five years he had set aside for civil practice.

Ramona's offense made the top of every list as 1987's "crime of the year." Not to put too fine a point upon it, she was charged with burning her husband Dieter's genitalia with a propane torch.

To Bea, Ramona was the archetype of all women who allow themselves to be victimized and shamed by men until self-preservation drives them to turn the tables on their tormentors. In an editorial in *Medea*, she claimed that Ramona was a person more sinned against than sinning. "Here is a man," she wrote, "to whom marriage had no meaning. From the first day of their marriage, he slept with other women. Within a month, he made his wife available to his friends." She hailed the case as a "test to see whether the state will allow women to protect themselves from abuse by the male of the species. A guilty verdict in this case will send the message that every woman in California is fair game for any man."

Bea is a colorful character and thinks more justly than she writes; off the printed page, she is thoughtful and soft-spoken. Once I looked past her purple beehive hairdo, her purple contact lenses, and her heavily rouged cheeks, I found her an interesting and charming companion. When championing the cause of women's liberation, however, she expresses herself in terms that would appall a political sound-bite writer. For example:

> Men are predators. They have feasted on the flesh of women for ten thousand years. They have designed the church, the college, and the workplace to condition women to think that their only function is to adorn men's leisure, to feed men's egos, and to serve men's lust. Our bodies belong to them. Our minds are formed to their needs. Our time is at their disposal.

> Men feel they have supplied all our legitimate needs when they grant us ballots and credit cards and driver's licenses. They remove our veils and caftans only to clothe us in miniskirts and pantyhose proving that our only use is as objects of their sexual desire.

And so on.

For the first and only time in my legal career, I was embarrassed to be associated in the public eye with a crime which screamed in bold type from the front page of every newspaper in the country. Other lawyers asked me with a leer whether I felt safe sharing the counsel table with Ramona; my golf buddies offered to make me a pair of asbestos undershorts. I suffered every joke about the case that occurred to anyone in the women's lounge or the men's locker room.

Copycat crimes abounded, each involving the same portion of the male anatomy, but employing only ordinary kitchen appliances. Once a crime elevates the perpetrator to the talk-show circuit, others piggyback on his or her format in the hope of financial reward or fame or both. It is a sad commentary on our society that a criminal act arouses more interest than a major revision of the welfare system.

"Why did you choose me?" Ashley asked Bea as the three of us met in the John Marshall Conference Room at Blackwood & Associates. "Why not someone like Gloria Wildfire? She did a great job defending Judith Boucher. Remember her? She cut off her husband's head."

"No, Ashley," Bea said, "we want the best, and we're willing to pay whatever it takes. But I want it clearly understood that you try the case, pure and simple, and no grandstanding."

Her intent was clear: she would do the grandstanding; Ashley and I would run the courtroom. Ashley found this division of labor acceptable; as I have said, it was one of his Rules never to talk to the media except to further his trial strategy. Bea, for her part, agreed to make no statements of a kind which might impair our defense. With this understanding and a meeting of the minds on the size of the retainer, we undertook the defense of "The Ball Blazer," Ramona's nickname in the tabloid press.

Bea fulfilled her part of the bargain. She raised the bail for Ramona and our retainer check arrived in a week. She recruited a guard composed of members of the Gloriana Society to watch Ramona's home around the clock. Any time a reporter came within sight of Ramona, Bea exploded with charges that the media were invading her privacy for selfish gain.

An editorial in *Medea*:

Here is a case where a woman has been used and abused by her husband. When she protects herself, the media degrade her acts to the level of snickers and cartoons.

What will it take to make the media respect women as equals? When will they consider that, just maybe, the degradation of a women is as serious a matter as the heel spur of a running back?

Has it ever occurred to the officers of the state that the person who ought to be prosecuted is not Ramona, but her husband, Dieter? He cheerfully admitted to having affairs with over thirty women the first year of his marriage. How many times did he bring to their home the pathogens of AIDS or the clap?

The man is a criminal, so why is Ramona being prosecuted and not him? Because the justice system of this country always punishes the woman, even though the criminal is the man.

At our first meeting with Ramona, I was struck by her pleasant and open face, silky brown hair, soft voice, lovely smile, and figure that, as a deputy said, "makes a man go weak in the knees." She grew up in Olinda, a small town in the Sacramento Valley. Her father raised artichokes; her mother was a cashier at the Woolworth store. As a teen-ager Ramona wanted to be a doctor, but she spent her high school years watching television and dating the football team and never progressed beyond eighth-grade skill levels.

When she reached eighteen, Ramona reconsidered her goals and decided that it made more sense to marry a doctor or lawyer than study to become one. She could achieve the same economic status with much less effort. Since Olinda offered a limited selection of single professional males, she moved to San Francisco and took a job as a gofer in a personal injury firm. For the next five years she ran errands, attended secretarial school, had numerous affairs, and met and married Dieter Krafft, a partner in the mid-sized firm of Jarndyce & Jarndyce.

Dieter, ten years her senior, was transiting his third divorce when he and Ramona started living together. He was a short, wiry ex-marine who shaved his head and spent two hours a day working through the steps of the Marine Corp's daily exercise program, supplemented by exercises he had invented to strengthen special muscle groups.

According to Ramona, Dieter had an insatiable appetite for sex. He insisted on intercourse with her at least twice a day and rigged a camera in the ceiling of their bedroom to record their lovemaking. When she discovered that Dieter was having affairs with other women, she begged him to stop, but he countered by stating that he wouldn't object to her having affairs of her own and named several acquaintances who were eager to spend a night with her. She acquiesced, she said, in the interest of marital harmony.

Ashley asked Ramona in a hushed voice whether she had received payment for her meetings with Dieter's friends.

She giggled. "No, not me. I never got a penny. I did it because Dieter asked me to. It seemed to make him happy, and I thought that if I did what he wanted, he would give up other women."

"Do you know whether Dieter received money for these encounters?"

She stared at Ashley with an open mouth. "You mean whether he got paid? Gee, I don't think so." She giggled again. "He said watching was enough for him."

Ashley and I looked at each other and then at Ramona. "I see," Ashley said. "Do you think it might have been his plan to blackmail them?"

"Who? Dieter? Oh, no, he wouldn't do a thing like that. He just wanted to show me off, show the guys what kind of a wife he had, that's all. He's always been a show-off. When he goes to a party, he always finds some excuse to strip to his shorts and flex his muscles. He can't help it. But the pictures were going too far. It was okay to tape him and me, because we're married, but what if Mom and Dad saw tapes of me with some other guy? I could never look them in the eye again. Plus he never gave up other women, like he promised. I got witnesses, real good ones, who told me everything. That's when I blew up."

"Meaning?"

"Darn it, I'd been a good wife and done all sorts of things for his sake that I didn't really want to do—I mean, making it with guys you don't know and him taping it— that's too much to ask of your wife."

"That's when you—ah—punished him?"

131

"Right! I acted all sweet and lovey-dovey and got him in the bedroom, which was easy to do, and then I tied him up—he likes that kind of stuff—and got him excited and turned on the video—"

"You taped it?"

"Uh-huh. He has this little gas torch he uses for plumbing, and I tied him and gagged him and put a baking sheet under his 'weapon,' as he calls it, so I wouldn't burn the sheets, then, instead of doing what he thought I was going to do, I lit the little torch and did his eyes ever bug out! Just before I gave him his first little burn, I said, 'This is for Pamela'—one of his girl friends—and boy, you should have seen him jump! Then I turned it on again and said, 'This is for Clarissa,' and I gave him another little burn down there, and so on, until I'd covered all the girl friends I knew about. There wasn't much down there I didn't scorch. Then I let him loose and he called an ambulance." She paused and gave us a lovely smile. "Do you think I cured him?"

Ashley swallowed. "I think so. Do you have the tape you made?"

"Oh, sure, it's in my purse. I thought you might want to see it." She smiled as she handed it to him as if expecting praise for her thoughtfulness.

"We better take a look at it."

I put the tape in the VCR and volunteered to go downstairs to the cafeteria and bring back coffee and soda and sandwiches.

Ashley stopped me. "No, Knute, we don't want coffee or soda or sandwiches, or peanuts, popcorn, or Cracker

132

Jack. We're not at a baseball game. You stay right here with us and watch."

It was the most painful half-hour I ever spent; it gave me nightmares for a week. Dieter was in agony. His jaw opened, he screamed and shouted and thrashed around frantically in his efforts to escape, but he was bound so tightly all he could do was arch his back and slam his head against the mattress. By God's mercy, the sound track was defective and his cries were barely audible.

When the tape ended, Ashley gave Ramona the usual advice to say nothing to anyone, walked her back to the reception room, and delivered her to the custody of Bea Benedict, who acted as her guardian throughout the trial. On returning to the conference room, he said, "Knute, you look worse than Dieter did." He poured shot glasses of brandy for each of us, and we downed them in one swallow.

"That was terrible," I said when I regained the use of my vocal cords. "No male will ever vote for her acquittal."

Ashley rubbed his chin. "Hmmm. Did you notice her expression while she worked on Dieter?"

I shook my head. I didn't want to admit that I had kept my eyes closed for most of the tape.

"She was smiling! Didn't you notice that? She had that lovely smile on her face all the time."

"I think my attention was elsewhere."

"As I walked out with her, I asked her why she was smiling, and do you know what she said?"

"I have no idea."

"She said, 'I was on television! You always smile when

you're on television.' That woman has the body of a goddess, but the mind of a ten-year-old. She lives in another world. Something's warped her."

"She's nuts, Ashley. Plainly and simply, she's nuts."

"Maybe, but I think there's something there we can use."

I guessed that Ashley had had another one of his insights, and I would have to wait until he revealed it in court, live and in full color.

As soon as Dieter was discharged from the hospital, he became a staple of both talk shows and news magazines. I would turn on the set expecting to see my favorite sitcom, and there would be Dieter grinning at his host and talking faster than a kitchen gadget commercial. He rattled on about his injuries, his affairs, and the exorbitant *honoraria* he received for his public appearances. He radiated the attitude, "Boy, I'm a clever guy to have done all this." No revelation about his character or past actions could shame him. He must have had remarkable powers of recovery. He laughed about his wounds, insisting he felt fine and would soon resume his active social life. Sports bars rocked with cheers when he proclaimed, "I'm even stronger now that I've been hardened by fire." He said he forgave Ramona for everything and looked forward to being reunited with her after she had paid her debt to society. "She's the best," he said on *Real People Talk*. "There's no doubt about it. What she's got, nobody else has got." He offered to sell the networks videotapes of her making love with him and his friends, and was disappointed when they declined his offers.

I asked Ashley if there was some way we could turn Dieter's insolent and brutish personality to our advantage.

"Let me think about it, Knute. Maybe we can work it in."

We deliberated about what judges would and would not be appropriate to preside over the trial.

"For one thing," I said, "it has to be a woman."

"Not necessarily, Knute. It depends on the woman. I can imagine some woman taking a very dim view of Ramona's sex life. She's a hot number. She had plenty of affairs before her marriage, and I'm guessing that she didn't mind having sex with those other guys. She just objected to the videotaping. There's no use trying to present her to the jury as your dutiful housewife."

"Okay, but a man's out of the question. Imagine him watching that videotape! What about an ultra-feminist judge?"

"That's it, of course, but it won't be easy."

I need to explain this colloquy. Ashley, as I noted in the *Lothbrook* trial, seldom had to try a case to the judge designated by the Master Calendar. The many favors he extended over the years to the judges and personnel of the court system insured that the judges assigned to his cases were those most likely to be sympathetic to his clients. A few months before Ramona appeared in the national media, however, a group of downtown law firms complained of the apparent favoritism shown to Ashley in the assignment of judges. Their attention prevented the clerk in charge of the Master Calendar from selecting any judge for Ramona's cases other than the one next up. The only way we could hope to obtain a sympathetic judge was to recuse—disqualify—the assigned judge, and hope that the next judge on the Master Calendar would have an outlook compatible with our theory of the case.

It is easier to amend the Constitution than to recuse a judge. The lawyer has to prove either that the judge has a conflict of interest or is grossly incompetent. Incompetence is nearly impossible to prove. Judges, even in the advanced stages of Alzheimer's disease, will never admit to falling short of the wisdom of a Solomon or the brilliance of a Brandeis. Proving the presence of a conflict of interest is no less difficult. A judge who is a member of the Klu Klux Klan and the American Nazi Party will not be disqualified from hearing a case involving an African-American Zionist. The attorney must show that the judge has a family or financial interest in one of the parties, or that there exists a personal antipathy between the judge and the client arising, for example, from defamation or battery.

The judge assigned to hear Ramona's case was Henrietta Mather. While a state legislator, she had achieved prominence by her opposition to abortion, divorce, and the Equal Rights Amendment, and she carried these biases with her to the bench. When a pre-sentence investigation showed that the defendant had a propensity to engage in salacious activities, she inevitably handed down the maximum sentence, no matter what the mitigating circumstances might be.

Ashley was aghast. He felt the case was lost before the jury had been selected. He knew Judge Mather would admit every piece of evidence prejudicial to our client and exclude any that was favorable. He moaned, "Knute, it will be a kangaroo court. We'll have to bargain a plea. Judge Mather would hand a person with Ramona's past a ten-month sentence for jay-walking."

"You don't think we could use self-defense?" I said.

"Not very likely, not when there's no evidence Dieter ever hit her, or even threatened to hit her."

"But there's the argument that he had all those affairs and God knows what kind of diseases he picked up and—"

"Knute, think about it. If everyone who's ever had an affair can be blown away by his or her spouse, a lot of people, including some judges, are going to start looking through drawers to see whether their partners have loaded revolvers."

I frowned and stroked my chin. "Well," I said, "I've heard of cases being tried to the judge and cases being tried against the judge."

"Yes, yes, yes," he said. Suddenly he sat as rigid in his chair as a judge dozing on the bench. He had fallen into his "trance" state. After several minutes, he rose and said, "That's an excellent idea, Knute. In fact, it's absolutely brilliant! That's what we'll do."

I apologize for inserting into this biography comments made by Ashley which seem to have no purpose other than my own self-aggrandizement. In truth, I mention this incident only to show how Ashley, great man that he was, never failed to compliment the members of his team for their contributions, however small, toward the success of a case. Regrettably, some journalists, misled by a few meanspirited men and women whom Ashley had to discharge for incompetence, claim that Ashley ate all the entrees and left his associates the breadcrumbs. Nothing could be farther from the truth. He gave credit where it was due and utilized his associates to the full extent of their abilities.

From the opening day of *People v. Krafft*, it was clear that Henrietta Mather viewed our client as a disgrace to her gender and ached for the moment when she could impose an extended jail term. Two women could not have been more dissimilar: Judge Mather, grim, bony, and sixty-two; Ramona, giddy, voluptuous, and twenty-five; Henrietta, learned and professional, a woman who had broken through the obstacles of the male legal establishment; Ramona, a woman happy to adapt herself to men's needs.

To my surprise, Ashley put Ramona on the stand. Her testimony consisted of embarrassed smiles and giggles to every question she was asked and saying she was sorry she hurt Dieter, but he deserved it because he didn't keep his promise to stay away from other women.

To lay a foundation for what would be his argument on appeal, Ashley asked Ramona on direct examination:

Q: [by Mr Blackwood] Please tell us, Mrs Krafft, how you spend your day.

A: [by defendant] Well, first thing in the morning Dieter and me screw.

[laughter]

Q: Well, after that.

A: I fix his cereal and mine and we catch the news on TV and eat breakfast.

Q: You both watch television?

A: Until Dieter goes to work. Then I watch alone.

Q: The news?

A: Oh, no. It's all talk shows and soaps and whatever's special.

Q: All morning?

A: Well, sure. Then I have lunch and run some errands, like the beauty shop, you know, come back and watch TV until Dieter comes home, when -

Q: Never mind that. How many hours a day do you guess you spend watching television?

A: All the hours except when I'm sleeping, of course, or listening to the radio or—you know what.

A: So, is it fair to say that your day is television?

Q: I can't get along without it.

On cross-examination, Sam Vishinsky, the prosecutor, tried to make her admit that at the time she was mutilating Dieter, she knew that she was engaging in a criminal act.

Q: You realized you were committing a crime, didn't you?

A: It happens all the time. So who cares?

Q: It happens all the time?

A: On *Top of the World* guys are always getting hurt, but they come back. It's no big deal. Same thing on *The Storm Riders*. All the programs. I never worry about the people. They always get well again.

Q: Are you referring to some television programs?

A: Sure. Don't you watch them? Everybody does.

Vishinsky tried repeatedly to make her admit she knew she was acting contrary to the law. Each time she came back with a giggle and insisted she knew Dieter would be fine the next week. The way she spoke, she gave the impression that Vishinsky wasn't quite "with it."

Judge Mather wore a scowl throughout Ramona's testimony. She addressed her as "Ramona" in a low, syrupy tone of voice, a clear breach of the courtroom etiquette which requires that judge and counsel refer to adults before the bar of justice as "Mr.," "Mrs.," "Ms.," or "the defendant."

Ashley and I never protested the judge's discourtesy, but Bea Benedict listed each affront in *Medea*. In fiery terms she questioned Judge Mather's competence to sit in judgment on a "real woman." She referred to the Judge as a "woman-baiter" and a "career sellout," language which, if spoken in the courtroom, would put her in jail for contempt of court.

In the end, Judge Mather's hostility towards our client served our purposes. There are two phases to any major criminal case, the trial and the appeal. A case lost in the trial court may be won on appeal. The most common means of obtaining a reversal of a conviction is to claim that some significant piece of evidence was improperly admitted or excluded by the trial judge. If the record reeks of the judge's animosity towards the defendant, the task of proving reversible error becomes less onerous. Far from imploring Judge Mather to extend the ordinary courtroom courtesies to the defendant, Ashley and I took steps to magnify her pique, nothing so obvious as to show disrespect, yet still enough to distemper her judicial steel.

One device we employed was to make lengthy and well-briefed procedural motions every day during the course of the trial. Judge Mather, like most judges, had ordered counsel to present all available motions before trial for the reason that, when a motion is made during trial, the judge usually has to suspend further proceedings until he or she rules on the motion. Most judges decide motions arising during trial from the bench, but a few, like Judge Mather, adhere to the legal tradition favoring protracted deliberation. If she chose not to make a ruling from the bench, she and her clerk would have to spend the evening researching the issue and have no leisure to unwind from a day in court.

We made incessant motions during trial so as to exacerbate Judge Mather's natural irascibility. We hoped she would deny a motion out of pique and provide us grounds for reversal by the Court of Appeals. In view of her order to file all motions before trial, Ashley and I were careful to provide arguments why the motion could not have been made at an earlier date. We also had to ensure that each motion contained enough merit to avoid the charge of frivolity, which could lead to a contempt citation or prejudice the appellate court against us.

Our volley of motions and *Medea's* barrage of epithets succeeded in flustering Judge Mather, with the result that she denied four meritorious motions. The most significant one was our request that we be permitted to exhibit to the jury the videotapes and audiotapes of all appearances by convicted criminals on television or radio talk shows during the last five years. The tapes and their transcripts filled six file cabinets.

Judge Mather responded to our request, lips curled in scorn, "Mr Blackwood, let me point out that, despite what you may think, this is a court of law, not a television studio. We are not here to sample the sewage pumped out by the mass media, but to decide a criminal matter. Motion denied." Ashley offered to reduce our request to only those tapes which Ramona had seen or heard, thus whittling the offer down to two file cabinets. Judge Mather once more denied our motion, and we made our "offer of proof."

In order to make a record on appeal, the attorney whose motion is denied must make an "offer of proof" to the judge out of the hearing of the jury. The offer outlines the evidence the attorney plans to present and demonstrates its relevance to the case. On appeal, counsel will argue that, if the evidence had been admitted, its impact might have resulted in a different verdict. If the appellate court agrees, the case is sent back for retrial with the direction that the trial judge admit the proffered evidence.

The trial lasted for another four days after Ashley's offer of proof, making a total of eight days, one of the shortest criminal trials of Ashley's career. When both sides closed, Judge Mather gave her instructions to the jury. After six hours of deliberation, the jury returned with a guilty verdict.

Ashley didn't seem disappointed. "After all," he said, "it isn't often that the state has a videotape of the crime dropped in its lap. But it's not over yet, Knute."

To our surprise, Judge Mather permitted Ramona to remain free on bail pending appeal. She may have reasoned that giving Ramona her freedom would stimulate second thoughts in the minds of any man who was toying with the prospect of engaging in an adulterous liaison.

When we argued for a mistrial before the Court of Appeal a year later, we were permitted to screen some of the videotapes and audiotapes which Judge Mather had excluded, after which Ashley spoke as follows:

"If the Court please, it is the contention of counsel for the appellant that the ruling of the Honorable Judge Mather on our offer to put into evidence the television and radio broadcasts listed and described in Exhibit M seriously prejudiced the defense's case. Her denial of the motion prevented defense counsel from showing that defendant lacked the required criminal intent because defendant did not understand that what she did was wrong.

"The evidence defendant offered, if admitted, would have shown that defendant is a child of the media age; that she does not live in the culture of the courtroom, but in the culture of the television set and the talk show. For all of her life, the only world she has known is the world which appears on her color television. The code we in this room live by has no meaning to her. She comprehends our legal system, our concepts of right and wrong, only to the extent they are enacted in one of her situation comedies or discussed in talk shows. We cannot judge her criminal intent, her sense of right and wrong, without considering how her acts appeared to her in the terms of her culture.

"Her culture, is not, Your Honors, our culture, the culture of books and newspapers, of classes and tests and graduation, jobs and wars and airplane crashes, unemployment, hunger, disease, and death. Her world is not the world Your Honors and I and the people who work in this great city experience each day. It is not the world of victory and defeat, of actions followed by consequences, of wrong-doing punished by fines and imprisonment.

"No, this defendant lives in the world of sitcoms and talk shows, where people act and talk for thirty minutes and no consequences follow. Next day or next week there will be another show with the same characters, and the story line will make no reference to the previous show. Someone's action or inaction in one scene never affects the following scene. A love lost in one sketch is followed by a new love in the next. A death today is forgotten tomorrow. All the players are immunized from the realities of life and death. All is laughter and high drama.

"So what are the principles of Ramona's world? That things just happen. Sometimes you lose, sometimes you win, but it doesn't make any difference, because the next episode is on its way. The past disappears into an electronic night. Nothing that has happened matters, because life will start over next week.

"A murderer who moves from our world to the television world with the blood of victims fresh on his hands, vies in witty exchanges with the talk show host. They chortle together like high school classmates who haven't met since graduation and can't wait to catch up on each other's doings. Embezzlers, con artists, convicts on death row auction their memoirs to the highest bidder. Murderers find fame; honest laborers die unknown.

"We submit to this Honorable Court that a person who lives in the television world cannot understand the concepts of right and wrong as we speak of them in the courtroom. A sitcom and talk show addict like Ramona cannot believe that life is serious, that actions have consequences. We call this Honorable Court's particular attention to the videotape of the acts charged to the defendant, and ask this Court to notice that throughout the tape the defendant is looking at the camera and smiling! *Smiling,* Your Honors! Why? Because she's on television! She is in that electronic world where no permanent injury ever results from an action. What she did to her husband appears to her as just another half-hour scene which will be forgotten by next week's episode.

"As counsel for the defendant, we insist that it was reversible error for Judge Mather to preclude the defense from demonstrating the mental state instilled in the accused by the culture of television. Lest the Court think we exaggerate the effect of defendant's world, we ask the Court to take judicial notice of a news item which appeared on the second page of today's *Examiner.* The headline says it all. 'Krafft Couple Together Again. Dieter and Ramona Reconciled.'"

With this dramatic flourish, Ashley sat down. The judges exchanged glances and were able to refrain from bursting into unseemly laughter only by the exercise of severe self-control. Six months later the court reversed Ramona's conviction on the basis that Judge Mather erred in excluding the television and audio tapes.

When I saw the decision, I rushed into Ashley's office to offer my congratulations.

"It was a stab in the dark, Knute. I read up on the judges and—what do you know?—two of them had spoken out in the strongest terms against television's glorification of crime and violence. I think that helped us."

"Do you think we'll hear again from Ramona?"

Ashley shuddered. "God keep her far from me. She gave me a bladder infection."

"What?"

"It's not what you suspect. It's because I kept my legs crossed all the time I was with her, and things backed up. Don't worry. I'm fine now."

I never felt a case was concluded until Ashley and I had discussed what Rule he thought had come into play. When I asked him, he laughed and said, "This one is pretty simplistic, but it worked."

"And it is—"

"IF IT'S ON TELEVISION, IT'S ALL FOR LAUGHS."

Sadly, our next major case produced nothing but tragedy.

A week before "Machine-Gun Marty's Massacre" in 1989, Ashley and I had a discussion with Mamie and Alexia which raised some of the issues presented by Marty's case. Ashley had invited us for dinner at *Pancho's*, the restaurant where the firm had held its "Thursday evenings" ever since our move to the Blackwood Building in Oakland. *Pancho's* was owned by Pancho Rellenos, alias Guido Malatesta, a jolly, heavyset man in his fifties who, along with his new name, had adopted a Spanish accent and a taste for Mexican cuisine. Ashley had defended "Pancho" on charges of statutory rape ten years ago. In gratitude for his acquittal, Pancho made sure that the service, if not the food, was four-star quality.

As we ate our quesadillas, Mamie asked Ashley a question she had often asked me. From her years of marriage to a lawyer, Mamie understood that every criminal is entitled to a vigorous defense, but she wanted to know whether he ever felt a stab of conscience for defending murderers who he knew from facts not admissible in evidence had committed the crimes charged to them.

Mamie never had the benefit of a liberal college education

and at times, I must admit, radiated a certain degree of what I can only characterize as antagonism towards Ashley. Whether it was the natural envy of an Iron Range high school graduate towards a successful and highly educated professional, or whether she felt Ashley deprived her of my time, or whether she shared the general frustration of the public over the workings of the criminal justice system, I cannot say. Her feelings, however they derived, led her occasionally into conversational skirmishes where she expressed herself to Ashley with more vigor than appropriate for a social gathering. I should add that Mamie, although not a scholar, has an ample store of mother wit.

"Ashley," she said, "let me pose a situation for you, what you lawyers call a 'hypothetical.' Let's assume you represent a serial killer and you convince the court to suppress crucial evidence on the grounds that it was obtained by an illegal search, and you get your client acquitted. How do you feel about being the one who sets him loose on the world? And how would you feel if the next person he kills is a friend of yours?"

"That's a good question, Mamie," Ashley said, "and there isn't any simple answer. So please pardon me if I take a step or two backwards in time. It used to be the law that evidence obtained by the police as a result of a search without a warrant could be admitted into evidence. The courts tut-tutted about it—"

"You're not answering my question," Mamie interrupted. "Knute's told me that story a million times. What I'm asking is how *you* justify the fact that you make your living by getting acquittals for men and women you know are guilty."

"The question is whether you support the principles of the Fourth Amendment."

"No, Ashley, that's not the point. But I'll put you a case that doesn't involve the Fourth Amendment. Let's say you stumbled onto evidence which clearly shows the defendant's guilt. What do you do with it?"

"Did I find it before or after he retained me as counsel?"

"After."

"The Code of Professional Responsibility requires me to do nothing. I can't turn it over to the police and I can't destroy it."

Mamie sighed. "I don't think you hear me. My question is, how would you feel if you got him off so he's walking the streets again?"

"I'd feel fine. That's my job."

"Really? As long as you do your job, you don't care what the consequences are to anybody else?"

"My job ends when the jury says 'not guilty.'"

"But what if your client guns down your best friend?"

Mamie is a tenacious disputant, but she lacks the logical approach instilled by a lawyer's professional training. Many legal practices which have evolved over the centuries for good and sound policy reasons, she views in black-and-white terms, devoid of their historical context.

Ashley maintained an affable air as he replied, "It seems to me, Mamie, that Nature and Society have cast us in certain roles without consulting our personal preferences.

One of our roles is to have children, if we so desire, but we can't control how they turn out. Some will become saints; some, mass-murderers; some, lawyers; some, executives. My role is to defend the accused, regardless of their guilt or innocence and regardless of the possibility that they may commit a crime in the future. Once they walk out of jail, I have no control over them. For all I know, they may get religion and minister to the poor, or they may bomb the Capitol. They could do anything. By the same token, the jury may convict an innocent man and send him to the gas chamber on the basis of perjured evidence. It's something no one can predict."

Mamie never gives up, even when she has lost. "Ashley," she said, "let me approach you on the emotional level, since you won't answer me on the level of ethics and morality. How do you *feel* when someone you defended kills again?"

"The same way I felt when he or she killed the first time. It's a great loss, a human tragedy."

"Would you defend them the second time?"

"Certainly, for the same reasons I just gave you." He allowed himself a smile. "Maybe, Mamie, I wouldn't be quite so dedicated at the second trial. I might turn to my friend Knute here and say, 'It's your turn this time.'"

Ashley laughed, but I could see that Mamie was dissatisfied with his response, even though he had said everything about the subject that could be said.

Marty Vickers achieved his brief notoriety on September 15, 1989. He was a letter carrier at the North Beach branch of the U.S. Postal Service. Until then, he, like so many other killers, seemed "perfectly ordinary" to his family and co-workers. None of them knew that his hobby or, more correctly, his passion, was collecting machine guns, not just the usual Uzis, Sten guns, Thompson sub-machine guns, and Schmeisser machine pistols familiar to our urban youth, but heavy-duty military pieces, U.S. M-60's, Browning Automatic Rifles, and Japanese Nambu's.

How he obtained them and how he paid for them on a postal worker's salary has never been adequately explained. The police speculated that he had intercepted checks of his addressees and forged endorsements. His sister, Jessie Vickers Colt, claimed that an inheritance from an uncle had provided him the means to pursue his hobby. I suspected that Marty was the perpetrator of a bank robbery in Pacific Heights for which an innocent man had been tried and convicted.

The deaths of Marty's victims were the product of so many blunders by the San Francisco Police Department and the postal service that I wondered why one or both bureaucracies didn't try to hush up the whole affair by "disappearing" the defendant. Had there not been a loss of fourteen lives, including the lives of two small children, the day of "Machine-Gun Marty" might have played out as a comedy of errors.

It staggers the imagination to think that this man could wander around the streets of San Francisco armed with three automatic weapons and not attract the attention of the police. But such was the fact. Or that, after he sprayed the North Beach branch of the postal service with over a hundred rounds, it took fifteen minutes before the emergency dispatcher notified the police that a heavily armed killer was on the loose.

Marty's rampage was the product of a trivial incident. On September 14, 1989, he was suspended from his job for two weeks with full pay. His suspension resulted from the postmaster's belated discovery that Marty had failed to deliver any mail for the past month; he simply dropped it in the dumpster of the first apartment building along his route.

For weeks before September 14, the addressees on Vickers's route had called Fred Farley, the branch post-master, and Beau Biddle, Vickers's supervisor, every day threatening bodily harm unless the problem was solved at once. When telephone calls proved fruitless, a deputation of some thirty residents appeared in Farley's office to de-mand an inquiry into the cessation of their mail delivery. Farley and Biddle promised that immediate steps would be taken to deal with the problem. Biddle called Vickers into his office and asked whether he knew of any reason for the complaints. Vickers swore that he had made his deliveries punctually and couldn't imagine what the prob-lem might be, unless someone was following him and emptying the mailboxes.

His answer satisfied Biddle. He wrote a report to Farley

a few days later saying he expected the situation would sort itself out with the arrival of new equipment later in the year.

The report failed to placate the public, and a delegation, this time of two hundred residents, stormed the North Beach branch at 9 A.M. and howled down Farley's and Biddle's explanations. That afternoon Farley received a call from Patricia Pac, the local representative to Congress and a member of the Post Office and Civil Service Committee. She threatened to relocate Farley and Biddle to Anchorage unless the problem was solved by the end of the week.

Spurred to sudden action by Representative Pac's concern, Biddle two days later ordered an immediate investigation and assigned Al Nader, a recent Harvard graduate, to commence a study of the service "impairment." Being new to the service, Nader failed to understand that what Farley meant by an "investigation" was a statistical comparison of the frequency of misdeliveries in the North Beach area compared to those in the adjoining areas. Instead, Nader shadowed Vickers and watched him drop the mail in a dumpster and unwind for the rest of the day at *Gipper's Sports Bar*.

Nader reported his findings to Farley that afternoon. Farley asked for a written report and was visibly piqued to receive it within the hour. He questioned Nader about any animosity he had towards Vickers, but desisted when Nader produced Polaroid pictures of Vickers emptying sacks of

U.S. mail into a dumpster. Farley dismissed Nader with
thanks for his investigative efforts, qualified by a directive
that "next time you better follow office procedures."

Farley and Biddle huddled over what disciplinary procedures, if any, to take against Vickers. They agreed that it
"looked bad" for him, but that Nader "had always been a
troublemaker, like all them Harvard types" and that "they
were stuck with a bad situation and it was no use trying to
put a spin on it." They spent the day analyzing 200 pages
of the service's regulations on procedures for "Compulsory
Leave of Absence for Medical Reasons." Since a disciplinary hearing under the Civil Service Rules would unsettle
office routine for over a year, they decided to avoid the
time and expense of a hearing and referred Vickers out for
psychiatric evaluation.

As they concluded their deliberations, Farley received
an angry call from Representative Pac inquiring about the
results of their investigation. Not knowing what Nader
might have told the other employees or the postal customers, Farley decided, after some hemming and hawing,
to read her the full text of Nader's report. When he finished, Representative Pac asked, "Well, what the hell are
you going to do with the guy? You're going to fire him,
aren't you? He committed a goddam federal offense!"

"Madam Representative," Farley said, "we spent all day
reviewing the compulsory sick leave regulations and we
decided—"

"Regulations? Compulsory sick leave? The guy's a
criminal! Get him the hell out of there!"

The next day Biddle, on orders from Farley, called

Vickers into his office and in the presence of a security officer suspended him for two weeks with full pay and benefits. Vickers insisted that he had done nothing wrong, that it was all junk mail, that he'd only done it once, and that Nader was a "Harvard smart-alec who has it in for me." Biddle tried to appear sympathetic, but Vickers continued to protest his innocence until Biddle realized there was no point in talking further and had the security officer escort him from the premises. As he left, Vickers muttered, "I'll get you for this, Biddle. I'll get all of you."

The next morning Vickers armed himself with a Thompson submachine gun, an AK-47, a Schmeisser machine pistol, and a backpack full of ammunition. He drove to the North Beach branch office, walked in through the unlocked employee entrance, and shouted for Nader, Biddle, and Farley. As luck would have it, Nader had been assigned to deliver Vickers's mail and, since it was a clear day, Biddle accompanied him on the route.

As he entered, Vickers stumbled over a mail sack and let off a few rounds from the Thompson. The employees hit the floor. When Farley heard Vickers shout his name and then the gunshots, he guessed he was in serious trouble. He locked his door and attempted to escape through his window. Vickers kicked the door open and cut him in two with a scythe of bullets. Vickers then turned and emptied the cartridge drum at the employees in the office, killing two other employees and wounding four. He put in another drum and left by the employee entrance.

The employees, except the dead and those too seriously wounded to move, fled the building without making any effort to summon the police or an ambulance. One of the wounded managed to crawl to the phone and call for an ambulance. When the ambulance driver arrived at the scene, he called 911 and told the operator that a heavily armed man was on the loose in the North Beach area.

Vickers wandered down Stockton toting the Thompson submachine gun in his arms, the AK-47 in a sling on his back, and the Schmeisser machine pistol in a holster at his hip. As he went, he sprayed bullets on both sides of the street, as if watering his backyard. One of his bursts ended the life of an elderly man being shaved in a barber's chair on the corner of Stockton and Greenwich and seriously wounded the barber. It was a mixed blessing that a recent flare-up of drive-by shootings had taught the residents of North Beach to drop to the floor whenever they heard gunfire, so that the fatalities along Greenwich were lighter than they might have been in a less battle-hardened neighborhood. The tragedy reached its height when Vickers's path brought him to the grounds of the Watson Elementary School, where some sixty children sported around their teeter-totters and swing sets.

One of the dispatchers at the 911 station was, by a malign fate, taken ill that day, and Dick Stentor, the supervisor, filled his position with a bookkeeper named Rita McNutt. Rita had acted as a dispatcher five years ago until the stress of the job drove her to request reassignment to bookkeeping. Since her transfer, the department had, unknown to her, installed new software in the system, so that a keystroke which earlier had activated a police response, now sent the message to an archival file.

Because a birthday brunch for the chief of the department had turned into what the press, with typical exaggeration, called a "bacchanal," Rita was the only employee available to fill the vacancy caused by the dispatcher's illness. Dick Stentor did not know that Rita had never been trained in the new system. When the call from the ambulance driver came to 911, Rita unknowingly routed it to the archives. Nobody summoned the police until she asked another dispatcher what the story was about the "guy who was shooting up the post office."

By the time the police picked up Vickers's trail at the Watson Elementary School, he had emptied the last drum of his Thompson, killing two children, one teacher, and wounding five other children. Vickers dropped the Thompson and switched to his AK-47, but found he had brought the wrong ammunition. He reached for his Schmeisser machine pistol just as two police cruisers, sirens blaring and lights blazing, raced down the street behind him. He opened fire at them, but the Schmeisser's recoil forced the shots high. He put in another clip and, aiming low this time, hit a police cruiser without injuring anyone. Officer Cody rolled out from the driver's seat and, as the bullets of the Schmeisser whistled around him, took careful aim and hit Vickers in the thigh.

The police had neglected to establish roadblocks around the area. Vickers managed, despite his wound, to commandeer a car from an elderly motorist who had driven into the area oblivious to the gunfire. Vickers drove back to his town house and set up an M-60 heavy machine gun in front, a Japanese Nambu at the back, and a Browning Automatic Rifle at the open side.

Fifteen minutes later a dozen cruisers crammed with police surrounded the area. Captain Oz Perry called on Vickers to surrender. He replied with a burst from his M-60 which killed five officers and wounded eight. The police withdrew and Perry summoned a tactical unit commanded by Lieutenant John Bullitt. Because of its much-publicized *elan* and premium pay scale, the unit's members were the envy of the department. They wanted to be considered fearless and charged the back of the house without checking its defenses. Twelve men led by Bullitt rushed forward with a cheer.

They ran into a spray of steel from Vicker's Nambu. Two men were killed and seven wounded.

Phil Guderian, the North Beach chief of police, replaced Bullitt and withdrew the troopers until they could obtain a light tank from the National Guard and "blast the fucker out of there." It was done that afternoon. The third shell set the house on fire, and Vickers walked out with his hands in the air.

Total casualties: fourteen killed, twenty-five wounded.

The public's fury over the incompetence of the police and the postal service expressed itself in editorials, graveside vigils, rock-throwing, and fire-bombings. Congress called for an investigation of the postal service; the governor called for an investigation of the police department. At present writing, both investigations are in progress, but a full report is expected before the end of the year.

When Vickers recovered from a bullet wound in his leg and the bruises suffered as a result of "accidents" which occurred during police custody, he asked the court to appoint him a lawyer. Because Marty Vickers was of African-American descent, Judge Manson appointed Otto Krabick as his counsel. Otto was notorious for utilizing the defense of "black rage" in any case where an African-American attacked an Anglo. Krabick's set argument was that the centuries of injustice inflicted by whites on blacks had conditioned them to see whites as natural targets of their rage. The crime, he contended, originated not in the mind of the defendant but in the history of his race.

"It'll never do," Ashley said to me one afternoon as we discussed the case in the John Marshall Conference Room. "For one thing, five blacks were killed and eight injured, plus juries, even all-black juries, are suspicious of 'black rage' arguments now. That's the trouble with a lot of lawyers—they don't see that each case is different. They think they can keep using the same old formulas, but juries love brand-new arguments, jazzy ways of looking at things." He pointed to one of the plaques on the wall: *TAILOR EVERY DEFENDANT A CUSTOM-FITTED DEFENSE.*

So much for Ashley's critics who claim he used the same defense over and over. He viewed each trial as a palette of facts from which to paint a masterpiece. Krabick's trials, by comparison, were the hack works of a calendar artist.

"It's just as well, Ashley," I said. "Krabick will botch it

and Vickers will be gassed, and we won't have to worry about him gunning us down on the street."

Ashley shook his head. "No, Knute, I don't think Krabick will end up handling this case."

"Why do you say that?" I asked.

"Just a hunch. The papers say Vickers is a very religious person." I was mystified by his answer until two days later when Ashley told me that Judge Manson had called and assigned him to defend Marty Vickers.

"Why?" I asked. "What happened to Krabick?"

"Vickers told the judge he couldn't get along with Krabick and wanted another lawyer. The judge didn't ask him for reasons."

The mystery lifted when we interviewed Vickers. Marty Vickers was a tall and powerfully built man, as he had to be to carry the weapons and ammunition he packed on that fatal September 15. Yet, despite his intimidating appearance, he was a man of modest manners and spoke in a low voice. "That Krabick fellow," he said, "he has a great big chip on his shoulder. Man, the language he uses! He can't order a cup of coffee without saying words that make me ashamed to be seen with him. I don't want a guy defending me that doesn't have any better control of his mouth than him. What if he talks like that in front of the judge and jury? I go to the gas chamber, that's what. He's already mad at the judge, and the trial hasn't even begun."

Vickers did not exaggerate. When I talked to Krabick about the change in counsel, he blistered my ear with language that forced me to turn off the speaker phone.

I couldn't understood why he indulged himself in these outbursts; surely, they must have hurt his career. No talk show host dared to interview him and no newspaper quoted him, so that he lost a great deal of free publicity. His manner of speaking may have been involuntary, a manifestation of Tourette's Syndrome referred to as "coprolalia," a compulsion to employ foul language in inappropriate settings. Or possibly Krabick thought that the language of the gutter conveyed a "tough guy" image that attracted the criminal type.

Ashley scoffed at this reasoning. "Criminals," he said, "don't want to be represented by 'tough guys.' A lawyer who talks like a 'tough guy,' is only a 'tough guy.' Criminals want a lawyer who knows all the tricks of the courtroom."

His homicidal tendencies aside, Vickers was one of our more personable defendants. He had a good command of formal English, groomed himself as well as prison life permitted, listened attentively, and remembered all we told him. He had a streak of delicacy that made him sensitive both to foul language and bodily odors. No doubt prison life tortured him day and night, but he never complained to us about anything other than the lack of inspirational reading material.

We had no need to review with him the details of his killing spree. The *San Francisco Chronicle* had documented each footstep he planted and each cartridge he fired, from the time he entered the North Beach station until he surrendered to the police that afternoon. Not even Ashley's fertile mind, I thought, could postulate a theory which would rationalize the murder or wounding of thirty-nine people, including seven children. Ashley admitted the case could turn out to be a loser, and told all of us at Blackwood & Associates that he needed our collective wisdom. Marty's case would be the sole subject of our firms Thursday evening at *Pancho's*. No one would leave until we had a theory of the case for Marty.

At Ashley's request Pancho prepared for us beef fajitas, refried beans and rice, steamed broccoli, salad, and his famous dessert tray. Ashley relaxed his prohibition against the use of alcohol during working sessions, and ordered a white Zinfandel to accompany the feast. "This once," he said, "I need your minds to float. I don't want logic. I want ideas, dreams, fantasies. We need a defense no one has thought of since Solomon. Unless we produce a winner, our ratings in California will drop to second-best."

Ashley taped us as we each proposed our theories for the defense. I advanced a concept of what I called "unconscious aggression." Nora Ganglia, our switchboard operator, came up with "involuntary attack syndrome." George Prentiss, our newest associate, suggested "temporal transference of the experiences of slavery."

The most important idea, although I failed to realize it at the time, came from Cecily Champagne, an office gofer. "Hello, everybody," she said. "Aren't we missing something? Like, what about the fact that all the police and post office people looked absolutely clueless? You know, like, the post office took weeks to find out where the mail was going. Then, hello, what do they do? They suspend the guy with full pay! And, like, the police! People are being slaughtered like medflies, and 911 puts on a dispatcher who's been five years on the beach. And, like, the police chief sends traffic cops against a houseful of machine guns! I'm not any lawyer, you know, but when you see that kind of stuff sticking to your hair, it's got to tell you the VCR's not tracking the tape."

The significance of Cecily's comment escaped all of us but Ashley. He sent us home to get some rest, but told me he didn't sleep all night thinking about what Cecily had said. He called me at five the next morning and told me to be at the office at six to swap some ideas with him.

"That's it," he said when we finished listening to Cecily's taped comments. "That's our defense."

"What is?"

"Knute, we lost sight of the first Rule."

"You mean, *IT'S ALWAYS SOMEBODY ELSE'S FAULT?*"

"Right, but here I think we'll put a little twist on it and say, *FOCUS THE JURY ON THE MISTAKES EVERYBODY ELSE MADE.*"

"You mean the way the Senate has a year's hearing to focus on how one guy maybe violated the political contribution laws, so people forget all about reforming campaign financing?"

"Right."

"That's the same argument you used in the *Tyler* case, isn't it, that Society pulled the trigger? I don't see how you can tag Society or anyone else with shooting those thirty-nine people."

"Of course, Knute, of course. Literally you're right. It was Marty's finger that pulled the trigger, no doubt about it. And the spree went on a long time. It wasn't exactly a knee-jerk response. So we have to turn the spotlight away from Vickers."

I still didn't see what direction Ashley was taking, but I went ahead with trial preparations, taking statements and depositions, retaining psychological consultants and jury advisers, searching police records, studying ballistics reports, and making the usual motions to suppress evidence. Vickers had no previous police record, and nothing in his background suggested a tendency to violence. He had been a bachelor all his thirty-eight years and had never had a serious or lengthy relationship with any man or woman. From all I could find, it seemed clear that Vickers had engaged in an orgy of killing solely in revenge for his suspension.

I told Ashley I didn't see any defense. "Look, the guy flipped when he got suspended, that's all. Insanity's the only way to go. Maybe the fact he's African-American...."

"Absolutely not. I told you that the 'black rage' defense is out of fashion now."

I didn't press the point. Ashley had made up his mind and was unwilling to explain his theory. Like an author, he wouldn't divulge the plot until he had completed the book.

When we visited Vickers in prison and asked why he trashed the mail rather than delivering it, he said, "Fellas, you'd know if you took my route some day. It's dog work. Ninety-nine percent of it is junk mail. You know who picks up the delivery tab, don't you? Us taxpayers. I deliver this junk, and next day it's sitting on the curb to be recycled. So I ask Postmaster Farley what he thinks about that. He is—was—a pretty decent guy, but dumb as paint. I ask him, 'How come letter carriers have to tote around fifty pounds of junk when it gets thrown away the same day? Is that a good use of our divine potential?' I tell him, 'You know, it makes me feel like one of them old donkeys down South that's tied to a pole and goes round and round all day turning the wheels of a cotton gin. It just isn't right to treat a human being that way.'

"Well, Farley gets all in a sweat and says it's the U.S. mail and we have to treat it with respect because it belongs to the government until it gets delivered, and we have the greatest government and country in all the world, and on and on. You see, the guy never hears what I'm saying. Maybe it's because I'm a black man and he's a white man and what I think isn't worth used toilet paper. He's a brain-dead political appointee and his mind's in the part of you that you don't ever want to get plugged up."

Ashley asked, "Is that why he didn't take any action about the complaints from the people on your route?"

"Sure, he couldn't figure what to do. He can't do anything unless he's done it fifty times before. He's a hundred-volt robot with a one-volt brain."

As we drove back from prison, Ashley seemed pleased about our conversation with Vickers, saying it had confirmed the validity of his defense theory. "It's the system," he said. "The system isn't working any more."

I nodded, although I still didn't follow his drift. I asked him whether he planned to put Vickers on the stand. "He's a rather appealing guy," I said, "and good-looking, too."

"Appealing doesn't count. Juries are scared to death of appealing killers. They're the guys who have a date with your daughter, and she ends up next day in the city dump raped and her throat slit."

At the trial Ashley let the state put in its case without raising any significant objections, but when he recalled the state's witnesses for cross-examination, he tore into them like a pit bull. Every government employee who had failed to act or acted recklessly was forced to confess that he or she bore some responsibility for the death of fourteen men, women, and children, and that, but for their acts or their failure to act, the toll might have been one dead, or even none.

The answers Ashley extracted from the witnesses evoked gasps of horror from the jury. As each witness stood down, the jurors shook their heads and exchanged looks as if saying "So that's the kind of government we get for all our taxes." I honestly believed that the admissions he dragged from Dick Stentor, the head dispatcher, from Police Chief Guderian, and from Lieutenant Bullitt would have led them, if offered a choice between sudden death and another hour of cross-examination, to go to their deaths with a smile.

Naturally, the state tried to limit Ashley's cross-examination, arguing that the blunders of governmental employees had no relevance to the crimes committed by the defendant. Judge Manson permitted the questions to stand on the grounds that the state on direct examination had questioned the witnesses in detail as to their observations of the crime and the roles they played on September 15, so that the defense on cross-examination was free to make its own inquiries on the same subject matter.

I think Judge Manson was on rather shaky ground here, and it crossed my mind that he may have enjoyed the spectacle of other public servants being roasted over a slow fire. His Honor had frequently been the object of pointed criticism by the Court of Appeals, along the line of the old saw, "This is an appeal from an order of Judge Manson, but there are independent grounds for reversal."

When Ashley finished drawing and quartering the prosecution witnesses, he rested his case without calling a single witness for the defense. In his closing argument he referred to his cross-examination of each of the state's witnesses, then spoke as follows:

"Ladies and gentlemen of the jury, September 15 was a sad day, a day of tragedy, of needless tragedy, a day that ended with the death of fourteen people who should not have died, the injury of twenty-five people who should not have been injured, all because the officials charged with protecting you and protecting these thirty-nine people, failed to do the job they were sworn to do. The concerted incompetence of these servants of the state turned what might have been a low-level disciplinary procedure into a capital case.

"Let us start at the beginning. Marty Vickers failed to deliver the mail he was supposed to deliver. If this small dereliction of duty had been properly attended to, none of the events of September 15 would have taken place. After receiving the first complaint, Postmaster Farley should have talked to the defendant, determined the nature of the problem, provided him with psychological consultations, and given him a medical leave of absence, if necessary. Either that or he should have assigned him a job less stressful than carrying fifty pounds of junk mail. If he had done so, the fourteen dead would yet live and the twenty-five injured would be well.

"But he did nothing. He did absolutely nothing until there was a crisis involving two hundred postal customers, the entire postal service, and the national Congress. At that point he suspended defendant without a hearing, contrary to all the regulations of the postal service and to all our notions of fair play.

"Defendant exploded, as any of us would, and launched an attack on the source of his problems. Did anyone at the postal station attempt to stop him? They ran out as fast as they could and never took the time to call the police or an ambulance. One of the wounded finally managed to crawl to the phone and summon an ambulance driver who called the police. You remember what happened to the message. It lay imprisoned in a computer system while lives were being lost in North Beach.

"I need not tell you the rest. I predict that you will remember until your dying day how Captain Perry sent five young officers to their deaths and eight to the hospital in an ill-considered raid on defendant's house. You will also carry the image of Lieutenant Bullitt sending two men to their deaths and seven to the hospital in rash attacks on a position defended by machine guns, a clear violation of all the rules of armed combat.

"In your deliberations, you will, I am sure, weigh Marty Vickers's actions and those of the postal service and the city police, and come to the only verdict justified by all the events which contributed to the needless death and injury on that fateful fifteenth of September."

The prosecutor made his closing argument that afternoon, and Judge Manson gave his instructions to the jury the next morning. The jury retired to deliberate at noon. As we walked back to the office, I asked Ashley whether he had any hope that the jury would find Vickers not guilty.

"Of course they'll find him guilty. Fourteen dead, twenty-five wounded. Do you have some thought they won't?"

"They have to, I suppose."

"Yes, Knute, but guilty of what?"

"Murder one?"

Ashley shook his head. "Manslaughter two—maybe one."

"But how can they ignore the evidence of premeditation?"

"Oh, they can't. That isn't the point."

"So, what am I missing?"

"The case is a trial of the system, as much as of Vickers. The jury's going to decide that Marty and the state are both at fault. They'll give each a little and take away a little. They'll compromise, like all juries. Instead of giving the state the murder one it wants and instead of giving Vickers the not guilty he wants, they'll settle in the middle, somewhere around manslaughter one or two."

"You're kidding."

"You want to make a little bet?"

I thought a minute. I'd won the office football pool the day before and felt that I'd used up my luck for the week. "No, I think not."

Ashley was right. The jury came back with manslaughter two, and Judge Manson sentenced Vickers to five to eight years.

Nobody was happy. The judge and prosecutor were furious because the jury had compromised a clear case of guilt. The press and media roared that Ashley had once more frustrated the course of justice. To my amazement, even Vickers was disappointed. He had been convinced by Ashley's argument that, when everything was said and done, he wasn't such a bad fellow after all and should be able to go back to his old job. Ashley was unhappy because he viewed any conviction as a mark against his record. It hurt a little more, he said, since he had tried the case on a *pro bono* basis.

But two months later he received a payment gratifying to his soul, if not to his wallet. Krabick had tried a similar case in Los Angeles using his "black rage" theory with the result that his client was sentenced to the gas chamber.

The world never rests. Two years later, when Ashley was swept up by a desperate scheme which nearly cost him his life, I was forced to realize that, in the end, we are all pawns of Fortune.

EIGHT

As I walked into the offices of Blackwood & Associates at eight o'clock on the morning of Wednesday, June 10, 1991, Nora Ganglia, our switchboard operator, stopped me and said, "Mr Olsen, there's someone on the line who's been trying to reach you. It sounds urgent."

I went back to my office as quickly as I could manage without seeming to hurry. Ashley always frowned at any appearance of haste. "Haste," he said, "projects an image of panic reaction. A lawyer should appear thoughtful and deliberate in all he does, not rushed and distracted."

I sat down in my chair and took a breath before picking up the receiver. "This is Mr Olsen," I said. "To whom am I speaking?"

A strident female voice snarled, "Never mind. We got Blackwood here and we want a million dollars for him — or he dies like a dog."

Some prankster, I thought, had managed to slip through Nora's screen, so I answered with a jest. "A million?" I said. "We think he's worth a lot more than that."

"Cut the crap, Olsen. We'd love to blow the fucker away, except he ain't worth nothing to us dead."

I wondered if my locutor might be Mamie using a disguised voice, but I couldn't imagine her using such language, even as a prank. I decided to stop joking and call the bluff of whoever was on the other end of the line. "Well, well, if that's the case," I said, "put him on the phone and have him tell me what this sideshow is about."

I heard noises of feet shuffling and something being dragged across a wooden floor, then a voice unmistakably Ashley's said, "It's me, Knute. They want a million dollars ransom. And they aren't kidding." The despair in his voice left no doubt that he was in mortal danger.

"Ashley! How in the world! What's happened? Where are they—"

I was cut off by the woman's voice. "Stop gabbing, Knute, and listen up. We want a million bucks in hundreds and twenties by the statue of El Cid in the Golden Gate Park at midnight tonight, or Blackwood dies."

"Wait," I said, "that's impossible. I tell you —"

She hung up.

I sat nerveless, the receiver in my hand, and stared out my window at the panorama of San Francisco across the Bay. I asked myself over and over, how could I rescue my best friend from this desperate situation? I took a big breath, called my nerves to order, and analyzed the possibilities in a lawyer-like manner. Insurmountable practical and legal difficulties seemed to stand between me and the fulfillment of the kidnapper's demands.

First, the firm cash account showed a balance of something over $200,000, barely a month's working capital. The bank would, I was sure, lend the firm amounts several times that on the strength of its income. Blackwood & Associates, however, was a sole proprietorship, rather than a partnership or corporation, meaning that its assets were entirely Ashley's property. No one else could borrow funds in the firm's name. I could, as an authorized check signer, draw cash from the firm's bank account, but that was all.

Second, I had no idea what assets Ashley owned outside the firm or where they might be. He had told me several times that I was the sole executor of his will, but I had never seen the will nor, despite my promptings, a list of the assets I would administer on his death.

Third, I had no way of knowing whether his assets were in a form which could be readily turned into cash, or in real estate which would have to be mortgaged or sold into a depressed market, resulting in huge losses to Ashley. In addition, both a sale or a mortgage of his property would require the services of title insurance companies, real estate lawyers, surveyors, and mortgage bankers. No lawyer or group of lawyers, no matter how highly motivated, could possibly close the transaction in less than ten business days.

Fourth, no lender would advance money without Ashley's signature. If the lender believed that the signature was the result of duress, such as the threat of death or bodily injury, the signature would not be honored.

Fifth, for a sale of stock, Ashley's signature would have to be attested by a bank or broker; a sale or mortgage of real property would require the attestation of a notary. Under the circumstances, I knew that no banker, broker, or notary would swear that Ashley's signature was his "free act and deed."

Sixth, a practical and not a legal point: the statue of El Cid was in Lincoln Park, not the Golden Gate Park.

All this meant that there was no way I could raise anything like the million dollars the kidnappers demanded.

These considerations flooded my mind within minutes after the kidnapper hung up. Fortunately, she called back a little later. This time I noted that the area code on my Caller Identification was 702, which meant Nevada.

"Knute, we changed our plan," she said. "It won't be the statue of El Cid."

"That's good," I said, "because there isn't any in the park."

"Right, so—"

I raised my voice. "Now listen here, whoever you are. I have to spell out a thing or two. There's no way I can raise a million dollars, or even a quarter million. Meet me somewhere and I'll explain the legal situation. After that, I'll bring you all the cash I can put my hands on."

"Quit stalling."

"You don't understand. I just can't do it. I can get you some money, but nothing like a million."

After a brief silence and what appeared to be a consultation with another person, the voice said, "Go to the phone booth on the corner of Van Ness and Clay at ten tonight and someone will call you. Your story better be good. Any tricks and Blackwood is history."

"Let me make something perfectly clear," I said. "This is cash on delivery. No Ashley, no money."

"You betcha."

"You're calling from Nevada. I want Ashley here in San Francisco unharmed."

"Gotcha."

I had promised Brutus to attend a den meeting of his Cub Scout pack that night. The thought of missing it saddened me, but the thought of explaining to Mamie an evening's absence chilled my blood. Mamie has a warm and untroubled nature, but when I am handling a discrimination case for a woman, as I was that week, and tell her I'll be home late, she subjects me to an interrogation more unpitying than any Ashley ever imposed on a hostile witness.

I told Maxine Gregg, Ashley's secretary, to cancel his appointments for the day and also the next day, saying that he had a debilitating case of flu. I searched his desk and file cabinets in a fruitless attempt to locate a financial statement. I considered searching the papers in his town house, but I had neither the keys to his locks nor the combination to his security system. I saw no alternative but to go to the FBI, explain my situation, and request their guidance. Given the professional antagonism between Ashley and the national and local law enforcement agencies, I did not expect a cordial reception.

The FBI's receptionist referred me to agent Conrad Javert, a bald man with the build of a professional wrestler, the voice of a bear, and the nose of a seasoned drinker.

"Well, well, well, Newt," he said, "so you're a partner of Ashley Blackwood, the cop-killer's best friend. Imagine your coming to us for help!"

"Actually, I'm his Fourth-Degree Associate, not his partner, and my name is pronounced 'Kah-nute.'"

When I told him of the phone call I had received, he said, "So, Newt, you think he's been kidnapped by some of the scum he defends? That's a bitch, isn't it? So, what do you want us to do?"

"It seems to me, Connie — "

"Agent Javert to you."

"It seems to me, Connie, that the FBI might possibly have more experience than I in matters of this sort. So I make bold to ask you, what course of action do you recommend?"

"Assuming you want to get the guy back alive—and it wouldn't bother me if you didn't—I'd say you pay up."

I started to explain to him the five legal difficulties—the confusion about the statue of El Cid having been cleared up—which prevented me from securing the ransom money. When I reached point three, he interrupted, "Okay, okay, he doesn't have the money or you can't get at it. Blackwood makes millions off the vermin we try to exterminate and spends it on drugs and broads."

"No, actually, he's very thrifty. But, Connie, let me be frank with you. If you feel a personal antagonism towards the law-abiding citizens you have sworn to protect, let me suggest you refer the case to someone in the bureau who can exercise professional judgment rather than personal pique."

"All right, I get it." He coughed and took a long swallow of some "cough medicine" he kept in his drawer. He called me "Knute," I called him "Conrad," and we addressed ourselves to business.

"Knute," he said, "you go to the phone booth like they said, and I'll have some agents keep an eye on you. The guys we're dealing with sound like amateurs, but that doesn't mean they aren't dangerous."

I drifted through the rest of the day in a fog of anxiety. I told no one but agent Javert about Ashley's abduction. I yearned to confide in Mamie, but I knew she would be concerned only for my safety and keep me in a locked room until Ashley returned unharmed or was found dead beside a highway. Instead, I told her that a case had been advanced on the trial calendar, and I had to prepare for an appearance in the morning.

"Is it that Muffie Farouk case?"

Muffie Farouk was an airline pilot whose story and picture had been in every newspaper in the past week. She had been discharged from Northwest Airlines on the grounds that her life-style after hours raised serious issues about passenger safety.

"No, no, dear. It's an embezzlement matter. Very serious."

My story raised Mamie's suspicions to Himalayan heights. "I hope," she sighed, "that your case makes you a lot of money. Your little boy Brutus will be upset when he hears you won't be at his Cub Scout meeting, especially since you solemnly swore that nothing would keep you from missing it. I spent all afternoon making a special dinner for us."

I was in no condition that day to see clients or prepare a brief, so I went to a movie in the afternoon, had dinner in the North End, and saw another movie before arriving at the phone booth on Clay and Van Ness fifteen minutes before the appointed hour of ten.

It was quiet that Wednesday evening in San Francisco. As I waited for the phone to ring, I watched bikers, pedestrians, and motorists pass by, and wondered if any of them labored under cares as heavy as mine, no less than the life or death of my best friend. How I acted in the next few hours would determine whether he lived and his firm survived. Nor was my personal danger far from my mind. Were the kidnappers a group of crazed drug addicts or just greedy misfits? Should I take their threat to kill Ashley seriously? If anything went wrong, would they dispatch Ashley and me by a shot to the head? Could I make them understand the difficulty—indeed, the impossibility—of meeting their ransom demands? And was the FBI in fact watching over me as agent Javert had promised?

I waited for what seemed like an hour until the pay phone rang. I looked at my watch. It was exactly ten o'clock.

There now began a two-hour series of exchanges between the kidnappers and me. Each lasted less than a minute since the kidnappers erroneously believed they could foil call-tracing devices by frequent changes of telephone locations. Most of the two hours I spent sprinting from one of several dozen phone booths to another.

In capsule form, our negotiations went as follows:

I picked up the phone after the first ring and said, "I need to talk."

"Make it fast." It was the same strident female voice I had heard in the morning. By her slurred vowels I judged that she came from Minnesota.

"All I can raise right now is a hundred thousand," I said. "Maybe a hundred and ten. It's all the cash there is in the firm account. Anything more will take weeks. You see, Ashley will have to tell us where his assets are, and then I'll have to get some lawyers and bankers to draw up the papers and get a notary to—"

"You're stalling."

"Most assuredly not. This is as important to me as it is to you. You see, you picked the wrong victim. If you're going to kidnap someone, you should pick somebody who has a family that can raise a lot of cash in a few hours. You kidnapped the wrong guy, so don't go blaming me for your own mistake."

I wondered whether this woman could possibly understand or credit my explanations, especially when she was predisposed to disbelieve anything I said and, judging by her *faux pas* over the statue of El Cid, seemed to have a few bells out of chime.

"You're shitting me," she said.

I thought it prudent to credit her sincerity. "No, I'm not. I know you're dead serious." Just then my mind completed a circuit. "Say," I said, "I bet you're Amy Bontemps. Didn't you take a shot at us by the Hall of Justice seven years ago?"

"Never mind who we are, Knute. We aren't messing around. What we want is money, and if we don't get it your friend Ashley gets snuffed."

It took me until midnight to make my five legal points.

I knew I had succeeded when she said, "Wait at Van Ness and Hemlock. We'll call back."

I went to the location she designated and, when the phone rang a little after midnight, she said, "Okay, you got a deal. Put $110,000 in hundreds and twenties in a brief-case and drop it in the trash barrel at the corner of Minnesota and 20th in Potrero Hill at nine tomorrow morning. Ashley will be there. We'll have you both covered. Any tricks and you're both dead. And good riddance. Got it?"

"Yes," I said, breathing a sigh of relief, "and I want to thank you for appreciating my difficulties. Not many people in your position—"

The connection cut off.

I debated going home for fear of the cross-examination to which Mamie would subject me, but spending the night in a motel or sleeping in the car would only confirm her darkest imaginings. I concocted a story about a client—not Muffie Farouk—being apprehended by the police on suspicion of murdering his wife.

"That isn't what you told me before," she said. "You said you had to prepare for a trial."

"Yes, I know. Both came up this evening. It's lucky I was in the office or—"

"Never mind. You've said enough."

Obviously, Mamie wasn't satisfied, but she did allow me a few hours of sleep.

Early Thursday morning I contacted Joan Cratchit, our bookkeeper, and told her to meet me at the office at 7:30. Before giving me a check for $110,000, she made me sign a requisition saying that all of it was to be applied toward Ashley's ransom. I'm sure she didn't believe a word I told her and suspected I was about to fly to Brazil for a permanent vacation from the law.

As soon as the bank opened, I presented the check and requested that it be paid in bills of twenties and hundreds, just as I had been instructed. The teller, Mattie Greene, and a vice president, Ben Keating, huddled over my request so long that I feared I would miss the nine o'clock deadline. There is a certain air of timelessness about bankers which irritates me when I am dealing with an emergency.

"Please," I begged, "this is a matter of life and death. If you have some doubts about giving me the cash, please call agent Javert at the FBI, and he can explain the situation."

"No, no," Keating said, "I'm sure, Mr Olsen, that everything is fine. You have the authority to draw a check in any amount on the Blackwood account. We're happy to be of service at a time like this."

I surmised that Keating knew of my status as a Fourth-

Degree Associate and wasn't about to quibble over my authority. I sighed with relief as I packed the money into an old briefcase, slid it under the car seat, and proceeded to Potrero Hill, satisfied that I had done all a man could do under such trying circumstances.

I parked the car at the corner of 20th and Minnesota and was about to drop my briefcase with the money into the trash barrel as directed, when a voice behind me shouted, "Freeze! Stay right where you are! FBI! Turn around slowly."

I dropped the briefcase and put my hands over my head as a precaution, although no such demand had been made. I faced a stocky woman in a dark pin-striped suit who held a pistol leveled at my head. When I turned, she must have identified me, because she returned her pistol to her shoulder holster and said, "You can put your hands down, Newt. I'm agent Krupke. Where have you been anyway? Didn't you hear the news?"

I shook my head.

"We got your boss out. He's not even scratched." I detected a tone of regret in her voice.

"You mean he's free?"

"You got it, Newt. Connie Javert sent me here in case you hadn't heard." She lit a cigarette and smiled as she inhaled. "It was a showpiece job, if I say so myself. Our people are really good. By 2300 we had spotted them in Reno, and by 0130 it was all over."

"Why didn't you tell me? I've been chasing around all morning."

She pointed her cigarette at my abdomen. "Javert said

you looked as if you needed some exercise. Besides, he wanted to rehearse the team a couple more times before going in. Like I said, it was a showpiece job."

"Are you sure Mr Blackwood's all right?"

"I bet he's back in the office right now figuring out how to let another murderer loose on the good people of San Francisco."

"Anything else?"

"You can read about it in the papers."

She handed me a copy of the *Chronicle*. Due to publication deadlines, the account added nothing to what she had told me. When the story appeared in the *Examiner* that afternoon, I found out that agent Krupke had omitted many details.

KIDNAPPERS FOILED BY QUICK ACTION OF FBI AGENTS; TWO KILLED; ONE WOUNDED

Famous Lawyer Blackwood Rescued

The FBI's vaunted "Black Beret" tactical squad conducted a daring midnight raid Thursday on a motel in Reno, Nevada, to rescue Ashley Blackwood, the well-known San Francisco criminal attorney, from kidnappers.

The kidnappers, identified as Edmund and Amy Mortimer, were both killed in a shootout with FBI agents. They had held Blackwood for an undisclosed amount of ransom since early Wednesday morning.

Fifty-two agents took part in the action. One agent was wounded in the shoulder and is in good condition at the Lazarus Memorial Hospital. Mr Blackwood was described as in good health, though exhausted by his ordeal.

The rescue operation was planned and led by FBI agent Conrad Javert. "Our guys are trained," Javert said. "They're not like the SFPD clowns who got shot up by 'Machine-Gun Marty.' We're the best."

In 1989 San Francisco police stormed a house defended by Martin Vickers, better known as "Machine-Gun Marty." In the fray, seven officers were killed and fifteen wounded, the greatest loss of life ever suffered by the San Francisco police in a single year. Mr Blackwood defended Mr Vickers in his trial for murder.

Ashley arrived at the office that morning about the same time as I. I urged him to take the day off and rest from the strain of the past twenty-four hours. He insisted, however, on staying until noon and asked me to join him for lunch. Naturally, I was curious to hear about his adventure.

"They had been following me for some time," he said. "I noticed a Ford sedan near my home several times last week. Now that I think about it, I should have realized it came from Minnesota. Even though it couldn't have been more than a few years old, it was rusted out and covered with bumper stickers. They must have learned that I went to the corner every morning to pick up the newspapers. As I cut down the alley behind the newsstand, the man and the woman grabbed me and put a gun in my back. I recognized Amy at once despite her disguise. I didn't know the man. She called him 'Ed.' The way she ordered him around, I figured he was her husband. There was a third guy in San Francisco they kept talking to on the phone, but I never got his name.

"They couldn't get the back door of the car open, so they put me in the trunk. It stank of fish. They didn't blindfold me, so I was able to look outside through a rusted-out panel. Minnesotans just don't have the knack for kidnapping jobs. All the good ones come from New Jersey.

"They drove a long time. I could see enough to know I was in Reno. They hustled me into a dingy motel and tied me to a chair and fed me a McDonald's hamburger every few hours. I felt a lot better when I figured they were negotiating with you."

"What scared you the most?" I asked.

"The FBI," he said. "There must have been fifty of them. They shot out the door and tossed in a concussion grenade. Fortunately, it knocked me to the floor. Their bullets were whizzing all over. I couldn't see or hear for a couple of minutes. It sounded like D Day. Amy and Ed must have been hit by a hundred rounds. If I hadn't been on the floor in the next room, I would have been sliced into stir-fry."

"The agents have been watching too many Clint Eastwood movies."

"It wasn't a rescue mission, Knute. It was a *blitzkrieg*. You couldn't walk on the floor for all the shell casings. The walls looked like lace curtains. Next time, Knute, tell the FBI to forget about rescuing me. I'd be safer with the kidnappers."

I asked him what he thought had driven Amy and Edmund to attempt a kidnapping.

"It's the same old story. They had good jobs years ago when he was a security guard and she was a bank teller. They began charging a lot of stuff to their credit cards and couldn't meet the payments. Gambling was getting big in Minnesota, and a friend sold them a 'never-fail betting system.' They lost their last nickel and began stealing from their employers. They got scared of being caught, and Amy came up with the idea of kidnapping me."

I told Ashley about my negotiations with Amy and my difficulties in explaining to her why the Uniform Commercial Code and the formalities of conveyancing prevented me from meeting their ransom demands. He was impressed by my summary. "So, how much did you end up offering them?" he asked.

"I got them to agree to $110,000. Not bad, considering they started at a million."

Ashley frowned. "Couldn't you get them down any farther?"

I smiled. It was time to apply a bit of levity. "No," I said, "I didn't want anyone to hear that your Fourth-Degree Associate thought you weren't worth at least $100,000." He wasn't amused, so I added, "But the important thing is that you're back, and you're safe, and your troubles with Amy are all over."

How wrong I was. The ghosts of the past never die.

As my experience with Javert makes clear, Ashley was not on good terms with the police and the FBI. Their antipathy towards him was rivaled only by their hatred of their own internal affairs departments. Despite the frequency with which he obtained acquittals of the accused and reversals of unfavorable rulings, our local judges and prosecutors did not share the antagonism of the police. Throughout his career, Ashley made a point of establishing cordial relationships with the judges and prosecutors he encountered in the courtroom. He invited them to social occasions, such as the open house we held to celebrate the dedication of the Blackwood Building, gave them tickets to athletic contests, contributed generously to their charities, sponsored barbecues at their schools and churches, and on their birthdays sent them a case of wine or hard liquor.

His greatest service to the judges and prosecutors was to defend them at bargain rates against charges of sexual harassment or driving under the influence, both chronic afflictions of their callings. At one time I listed not less than fourteen judges and twenty-two prosecutors he had defended on one or the other charge, or both, always with favorable results.

To Ashley it was a matter of principle. He felt that prosecutions for drunk driving and sexual harassment constituted unwarranted intrusions into the lives of the citizens of a free country. "These are not ordinary men and women," he said. "These are professionals who live under enormous stress. If work pressures sometimes push them out of bounds, we should make allowances."

Another reason for his popularity with the bench and

bar was that Ashley had a Rule: *NEVER MAKE AN ENEMY UNNECESSARILY.* When faced with an incompetent judge or prosecutor, he took pains to ensure that, while winning the case for his client, he did nothing to embarrass the men or women on the bench or at the prosecutor's table. As they matured in their careers, they contrasted Ashley's courtesies with the scorn heaped on them by less thoughtful members of the Bar.

Never one to live by a single Rule, Ashley had developed a corollary Rule: *FOR STRATEGIC REASONS YOU SOMETIMES HAVE TO MAKE AN ENEMY.* This Rule was exemplified by our encounter with Angelo Manzoni, the head of the infamous Clementi crime "family."

As I said earlier, Ashley refused under any circumstances to represent a member of the Mafia because of the devastation which their trafficking in drugs visited upon the youth of our country, so I was astonished when he called me into his office to meet Angelo Manzoni.

Angelo was famous for the attention he paid to his personal grooming in an effort to escape the stereotypical Sicilian Mafioso look. His face was at all times cleanly shaven and as pink as that of a boy of ten. The tailored shirts and suits which swathed his portly figure were always freshly pressed. Gold rings, cuff links, watches, and bracelets gleamed around his wrists and fingers. His shirts were monogrammed in large gothic letters, and his shoes shone like patent leather. The press referred to him as "Manzoni the Magnificent." To me he looked like an upright Easter ham glazed with sugar and studded with cloves.

As I walked into Ashley's office, Angelo nodded at me, jerked a thumb over his shoulder in the direction of two huge men who stood on each side of the door as silent and motionless as palace sentries, and growled, "Little Joe and Cruncher."

Ashley leaned back in his chair, steepled his fingers, and said to me, "Mr Manzoni here would like us to represent him on a business matter, Knute. He hasn't yet told me the nature of his project."

Angelo closed his eyes momentarily, as if stricken by the evils a wicked world imposes upon the righteous. When he spoke, his voice sounded like the growl of a lion with a sore throat. "I tell you, the DA's got a stool stuck up his ass about—"

Ashley waved his hand to stop him. "Mr Manzoni, if you wish to tell us something of a confidential nature, you must first dismiss Little Joe and Cruncher."

Angelo jerked his head, and the two giants stepped out of the room with the grace and agility of ballet dancers. He cleared his throat, but there was no discernible improvement in the quality of the sound he produced. "I'm hearing," he said, "that the DA thinks I was involved in some happenings down on Brannan."

He was referring to an incident of the previous week when a cloud of bullets minced the bodies of two rival mobsters of the Braganza family and three bystanders in a restaurant in the South of Market area.

Ashley nodded. "So I've heard."

"Not my deal," Angelo said. "I don't know nothing about

it. Weren't my guys, not my territory. Probably some heavies from LA. Not a San Francisco operation. Not the way people do it here. No restaurant shoot-ups, not since the 50s. You could kill a cop and get into trouble."

Angelo gave me the impression that, as an artist in his field, he felt obliged to distance himself from the work of amateurs.

"So, it was a complete surprise to you, Mr Manzoni?" Ashley asked. "You know absolutely nothing about it except what you read in the newspapers?"

"Well, yah, you got it. Hell, we don't know nothing about those guys or what they was doing up here. I wasn't even in the country. I was taking time off to see my family in Palermo. A guy's got to rest, you know. I love my work, but it gets to me sometimes."

"I understand, Mr Manzoni. Don't say anything more right now. I have some friends in the precinct who owe me some favors. I'll go there today and find out what kind of story is floating around and put every man and woman in the firm on the job. How does that sound to you?"

Angelo grunted, stood up, and dropped a packet of bills secured with a rubber band on Ashley's desk. I assumed this was our retainer. Ashley let it lie on his desk and avoided looking at it. When Angelo left, I summoned the bookkeeper to take it away. "Put it in trust funds," Ashley said. "I don't want it on the firm books."

"You're not taking the case?"

"No, of course not. The money would be nice, but if I take him on and we win, he'll ask me to take on more cases, and I don't want to be tied to a guy who sells coke and runs whores. It makes it too easy for the cops to manufacture a case and keep me out of circulation."

"So, why don't you just tell him you can't take it?"

"Knute, my friend, Angelo Manzoni is not the kind of guy who takes no for an answer. Got any ideas how we get out of this one?"

"I suppose we could take the position that we have to follow legal ethics, and if he tells us something we know is false, we can't put him on the stand."

"Put him on the stand? Knute, no attorney has ever put Angelo on the stand. The guy's a compulsive liar. If we put him on, he'll think he's up there to amuse the judge and jury with some of his stories. You'd start bargaining a plea after a half-hour of direct examination. No, Knute, that's too obvious. Angelo would see through it in a flash. Let's be a little more subtle." He thought a moment. "How about being so eager we frighten him?"

I shook my head. "What do you mean?"

"Those gunmen weren't from LA. They were Angelo's own men pretending to be some LA drive-by types. When you take a close look at it, it was a nice, clean job. He threw in the death of some bystanders to make it look sloppy. You can bet that when everything points away from Angelo, it's his." Ashley smiled. "It might be enough to fool the cops back in Minneapolis, but they're too smart out here."

"So what's your plan?"

"We blanket the town with investigators, interview all

the witnesses, talk to everyone in the Manzoni family, pore over his telephone logs, check his diary, do lab tests—the whole deal. We make sure word gets back to Angelo right away that his lawyers are looking at every single thing he's ever touched. He'll fire us in minute. It will cost us, but it's money well spent. Call it health insurance."

"I get it. Angelo fires us before we can get anything on him."

"Right, Knute. So what do you think?"

"It's masterful. When do we start?"

"Tomorrow early. I'm putting you in charge."

I sent out three trained investigators to learn all they could about the victims and about Angelo's associates, and to build a log of their movements for the past month. I told another four to interview all the district attorneys and police officers who had ever investigated Angelo or his business connections.

That afternoon Angelo summoned Ashley and me to his suite in the Fairmont Hotel and, as soon as we entered, bellowed, "What the hell are you doing, Blackwood? Everybody I met in my whole goddam life, and a lot I never heard of, tell me your people want to talk to them. Whose side are you on, anyway?"

Angelo was accompanied by Little Joe, Cruncher, and his only son, Erculano, a pale, skinny lad of twenty-four years with the beak of a parrot. Erculano had just been admitted to the Bar in a private ceremony presided over by Chief Justice Manton of the supreme court and blessed by Cardinal DeSapio. Throughout our meeting, Erculano's expression remained frozen in a scowl which implied that no one was going to put anything over on him.

Ashley rose from his chair and said with a hurt look, "Angelo, please. I'm pained by your question. I'm your attorney. I'm on your side."

"Yeah, well, you ain't doing what my attorney is supposed to do, which is to tell the police it's a bum rap and get them off my back."

"Of course, Angelo, of course. That's what we're doing. We're conducting our own investigation. You wouldn't want us to accept the police reports and say that's the way it went down, would you?"

"Shit! What d'ya need to talk to my people for? I can tell you whatever you want to know. You don't have to go nosing around. You want some witnesses, I'll get you some witnesses."

"Angelo, I can't defend you unless I know the facts, and I can prove them. Just because you tell me something is true, doesn't mean that it's evidence I can use at the trial."

Ashley looked at Erculano for confirmation. Erculano was eager to be viewed as a lawyer of Ashley's stature and said in a reedy voice, "That's right, Papa. Mr Blackwood has to have facts that can be admitted under the rules of evidence."

Angelo growled. "Well, I don't like it. No legal eagle's ever done this to me before. I'm telling you, Blackwood, you're getting on my nerves. Maybe you ain't the kind of lawyer I need."

Ashley's face reflected sorrow and injured pride.

"Angelo, it would be a blow to me to lose a valued client like you. You're a businessman. You know how to run your organization. That's how you achieved your high standing in the community. I work the same way. If I do a job, I do it right. It's the only way I ever do a job. Talk to Erculano here, and you'll see that I'm following approved legal procedures."

The look on Angelo's face implied that he wasn't about to discuss anything with Erculano. The next day we received a letter from Jonathan Wild, a criminal attorney who specialized in intimidating witnesses and bribing jurors. The letter stated that Angelo was terminating our representation and enclosed a directive signed by Angelo to return our files and his retainer.

We packed up the files and sent them to Wild along with the full amount of Angelo's retainer. As Ashley signed the transmittal letter, I said, "I bet you have a Rule for this situation."

"Right, Knute: *NEVER TURN DOWN ANYONE WHO CAN HURT YOU; MAKE HIM TURN YOU DOWN.*"

Ashley's handling of Angelo stands as one more proof that he never took a case he didn't believe in. He could have represented many more people and harvested many more retainers, but his principles kept him from taking the easy way. His Christian conscience cost him a fortune, he said, but it never cost him a moment's sleep.

NINE

After the "Machine-Gun Marty" case, Blackwood & Associates had no cases that attracted the attention of the national media until April 10, 1992. On that day hockey fans at an exhibition match in the Cow Palace watched with horror as two long-time rivals, Mikhail ("Mick") Milosevich, left wing for the Saskatchewan Sachems, and Henri Laval, right wing for the Trois Rivières Terreurs, battered each other on the boards until Mick fell to the ice unconscious.

Several years have passed since the *Laval* case, and people now cannot comprehend the public's fascination with the investigation and the trial. Whenever a new witness appeared on the television, office work paused, assembly lines slowed, and passengers throughout the civilized world missed their flights. On the promise of more revelations, tabloids scorned by anyone with an elementary school education, sold out at office buildings and university campuses across the country.

The *New York Times* estimated that the television, newspaper, and magazine industries hired an additional 2800 employees to supply direct and background coverage. Sports bars installed television sets dedicated to the *Laval* trial. When a speech by President Bush interrupted crucial testimony, his popularity rating dropped eighteen percentage points. Americans, from professor to peasant, debated the guilt or innocence of Henri with the sophistication of Minnesota Law School graduates.

In every major city at least one channel carried full-time coverage of the courtroom proceedings. A dozen law school professors took their families on Caribbean cruises with the income they received from expressing instant opinions on the testimony of the day. Jurors and witnesses sold their "stories" and bought new cars or houses from the proceeds. The district attorney's office added sixteen attorneys and paralegals to the prosecution team, while the county hired forty uniformed officers to keep order in and around the courthouse. Legislators bewailed the extra burdens on the public treasury.

Blackwood & Associates added one switchboard operator.

The demands of the media for "inside" information knew no restraint. Ashley's assistants managed to keep him far from the public clamor, but I was besieged hourly by reporters and camera crews who implored me to say something, anything, about Henri, Ashley, Mick, or myself. They offered me thousands for a scrap of biographical data on anyone connected, however tenuously, with the case. One attractive television anchorperson hinted she would trade—not to put too fine a point upon it—her sexual favors for hints about our defense strategy. Maddened by the incessant begging calls, many overtly salacious, Mamie changed our phone to an unlisted number.

In fairness to the media, no fan who attended the game will ever forget it. I speak with authority, since Brutus, Alexander, and I sat in the fifth row center. Henri had just been sent to the penalty box for high-sticking. Mick led the Sachems to a goal in the last seconds of the power play giving them a 3-2 lead over the Terreurs early in the third period. The instant his penalty expired, Henri raced back to the ice and within seconds checked Mick against the boards. They exchanged punches and, before the referee could separate them, Mick lay motionless, facedown on the ice. Two Sachems attacked Henri. As if on cue, players on both benches rushed to the ice to slug and slash the opposing players.

While the referees attempted to part the combatants, Ivan Kutuzov, the coach of the Sachems, noticed that Mick showed no signs of rising to his feet. He grabbed the team's medical doctor, and the two of them waddled across the ice and knelt by Mick's side.

The audience's interest shifted from the melee to the three men beside the boards. The medical director cupped his hand over Ivan's ear and whispered a few words. Ivan grabbed a passing Sachem player between brawls. The player sped to the bench and spoke to an assistant coach. Three paramedics in white uniforms rushed over the ice to Mick's side. At the urging of their coaches and the referees, the players on both teams returned to their benches. A hush fell over the arena. Two more medics brought a stretcher and gurney and wheeled Mick off the ice. When play or, rather, combat resumed, the Sachems, inspired by the thirst for revenge, swept to a 5-3 victory.

Mario Evangelista, the announcer in the arena, said that Mick was being taken to the hospital, and he promised to keep the spectators informed about his condition. The audience on national television, however, already knew that Mick was dead. For their entertainment Channel Six played and replayed his last minutes on earth.

Medical experts summoned by the networks guessed at the cause of his death. Since the camera angle and the boards prevented a clear view of the exchange of blows, they speculated that death could have been caused either by trauma or by a spontaneous event, such as a stroke or myocardial infarction. Television anchors droned that "injury and death are running mates of all contact sports," that "Mick's death is yet another example that even games can be for keeps," and similar platitudes too tiresome to bear repetition. On television Henri expressed with tears his regret over "the *accidente tragique* which has lost to us the noble Mikhail, a player with the *coeur* of a *lion de France.*"

The day after the game, Ashley surprised me by saying, "I bet it isn't over yet, Knute, not by a long shot." What he knew or how he knew it, I never learned. I often thought he had a special sense that allowed him to detect oncoming events, the way crabs shelter in tidal marshes days before the arrival of a hurricane. "There's something there,

Knute," he said. "I don't know what it is, but I have the feeling that we will be hearing a lot more about Henri Laval."

"You think it wasn't an accident?"

"I don't know what to think about it, but it doesn't seem logical to me that a hockey player, armored like a medieval knight, would get killed in a fist fight, and I can't believe he had a stroke or a heart attack."

Ashley knew less about hockey than I know about molecular biology. I told him of several Iron Range games I had participated in where players suffered serious injury in a brawl. Mick's death was accidental, I insisted, a consequence of the *joie de vivre* bred by sporting contests.

"No, Knute," Ashley said, "I watched the TV tape of the game and I saw how professionals fight. It's sort of stylized, like a Japanese play, isn't it? They put on a good show and look tough, but at bottom they don't want to get benched for injuries. I bet if you watch carefully, you'll see there's a big difference between the way professionals and amateurs fight."

I had learned not to argue with Ashley when he'd made up his mind. And I'm glad I didn't, because later that week I spoke to my friend Sergeant Kesselring of the San Francisco police, and he told me the incident was under investigation. A team of detectives had uncovered some facts which indicated that there was more at issue between Mick and Henri than a sporting rivalry.

Sergeant Kesselring asked me to treat the information as confidential, so imagine my surprise when I saw the following story in the *San Francisco Chronicle*:

MORE THAN A PUCK?
AN OFF-ICE RIVALRY

by Priscilla Quill

The San Francisco Police Department and the Royal Canadian Mounted Police are investigating rumors that the rivalry between Henri Laval and Mikhail Milosevich was not confined to the hockey rink.

According to reliable sources, Laval believed Milosevich was having an affair with his wife, Juliette, and had sworn vengeance *"a outrance."*

Now that sex had joined with murder and sports, the *Laval* case exploded into an international *cause célèbre*. Reporters rose from the earth like the clouds of mosquitoes which emerge at dusk from the Minnesota wetlands and arrived in chartered planes on the Canadian taiga, ravenous to suck from the spouses, ex-spouses, parents, siblings, teammates, cousins, and neighbors of Mick and Henri the details of their sex lives. They discovered that Mick and Henri, though happily married, spent many of their spare hours on the road in the company of female "hockey groupies" anywhere between puberty and menopause. Hundreds of women volunteered to Priscilla Quill, the *Chronicle's* social page reporter, "true stories" of the ins and outs of their liaisons with Henri or Mick or both, revelations which must have provided painful reading for their families and fans. Most of these informants, in my opinion, claimed an intimacy to which they had no title and exposed themselves solely in the hope of obtaining pictorials in *Playboy* and other publications which appeal to prurient interests.

Mick's wife, Justine, incurred the media's wrath by leaving Saskatoon and moving herself and her children to a Cree village in northern Saskatchewan. Reporters and photographers were dismayed to find on arrival that there was no lodging, electricity, or hot water, and that the only potable spirits were native concoctions which induced out-of-body experiences of abduction by three-eyed aliens. To add to their frustration, Justine gave no interviews and refused to comment on the rumors of Mick's extra-marital relationships. The few who endured the hardships of the *pays haut* spent their idle time composing human interest stories of village life.

Laval's wife, Juliette, by contrast, gave press conferences from her home in Trois Rivières on a daily basis. She denied having had any inappropriate relationship with Mick or Mick's or Henri's teammates, but offered to sell her story to the major magazines.

A few weeks later Ashley called my attention to the following item in the *San Francisco Chronicle:*

MORE MYSTERY:
WAS LAVAL'S STICK FIXED?

by Lon Shade

Serious doubts have arisen about the manner of the death of Mikhail ("Mick") Milosevich, left wing of the Saskatchewan Sachems, who died during a scuffle with Henri Laval during an exhibition game played here on

April 10. Laval was a long-time rival of Milosevich in the Canadian hockey standings.

The autopsy report of the San Francisco medical examiner stated only that Mick had died of an aneurysm. However, an undisclosed source at the police department said today that a player for the Sachems told him that he had picked Laval's hockey stick off the ice, and it felt as if it had been weighted with lead.

The police are reviewing the videotapes of the game for any evidence of a lethal blow to Milosevich's head.

"Ashley," I said, "your insights never cease to amaze me! What's going to happen next?"

"I bet they'll find Henri's stick this week, if they haven't already."

Lon Shade's article ignited an internecine feud among the staff of the *Chronicle*, a battle which continues to this day. Lon had been a crime reporter for the *Chronicle* for fourteen years. Priscilla Quill resented his article on Laval's hockey stick as an invasion of her private journalistic domain. She claimed that she had written the first piece revealing the possibility that the death of Mick might not have been accidental, and therefore she should have the exclusive right to any succeeding stories. Shade responded that crime was his province and that Quill, a "society reporter," would embarrass the paper by her ignorance of criminal procedure. "My fellow reporter Priscilla," he wrote, "doesn't know the difference between an arraignment and an indictment. Readers, be warned: don't credit any facts she puts into print until I give you the real information in my column."

Tom Punt, the paper's lead sportswriter, joined the fray by stating that Shade and Quill had no business writing about sports figures. Anything that occurred on turf, ice, clay, or wood, Punt claimed as his province. "Shade and Quill know nothing about the game of hockey. They think a cross-check is a polite way of saying 'insufficient funds' and that an 'icing' call signals a time-out for refreshments."

To show that he knew his way around a crime scene as well as Shade and Quill, Punt went to press with two revelations:

TWO VITAL CLUES UNEARTHED
IN MILOSEVICH DEATH;
EVIDENCE IMPLICATES LAVAL

by Tom Punt

This reporter has learned that a partially burned hockey stick has been found in an alley behind the Brahma Motel in Regina, Saskatchewan. The stick bears the logo of the Trois Rivières Terreurs and the initials HL. The upper half of the stick had been hollowed out and filled with lead, making it a formidable weapon.

The Terreurs played a game in Regina two days after the death of Milosevich and lodged at the Brahma Motel.

Emil Edison, a Fresno hockey fan, told this reporter that he had taped parts of the April 10 game, including the duel between Milosevich and Laval. The tape is said to show Laval in the act of delivering a blow to Milosevich's head, followed by Milosevich's fall to the ice.

Both of these crucial pieces of evidence have been overlooked by other reporters and investigators, including the San Francisco Police Department and the Royal Canadian Mounted Police.

Smarting from this scoop, Quill and Shade demanded that the publisher give him or her the exclusive coverage of the story. The publisher could never make up his mind whom to prefer, so whoever had the better story by press time won the front page space. The result was that the slant on the case and even the facts changed from day to day, depending on whose story appeared. Given the disarray in the press, it is no wonder that the public throughout the trial had an unusually confused perception of the underlying facts.

Sylvia Ames, a prominent Harvard Law School professor, questioned whether or not the case should be tried in the courts. She contended that Mick's death was a natural incident to the game of hockey. "Every player," she wrote, "takes the risk that any of the melees so dear to the game may get out of hand and result in serious injury or death. If a player violates the rules of the rink, he should be punished in accordance with the procedures of the Canadian Hockey League, not the courts."

The league addressed the issue at a contentious meeting. Rumor had it that two of the owners came to blows. When two pucksters disagree, custom seems to require that they resort first to fisticuffs. At the end of its session, the league adopted a resolution to the effect that what happens to players during a contest is none of the state's business.

That ruling prompted a Pacific Heights attorney to write to the *San Francisco Examiner*:

> What is this game of hockey? Is it a sport or a gladiatorial contest? Having inured ourselves to the reality that players are thugs rather than sportsmen, are we now to give them a license to kill?
>
> Our schools spend millions teaching children the fundamentals of sportsmanship, fair play, and honest competition. Should we fire our hockey, football, basketball, and baseball coaches and hire in their stead disciples of Machiavelli and Lenin?

Skip Robespierre, district attorney for the City and County of San Francisco, responded in a press release stating that "murder in the course of a sporting event is still murder, and it will be vigorously prosecuted by this office."

Ivan Kutuzov, Mick's coach, hired his own expert to review the medical examiner's report. A week later the medical examiner issued a revised autopsy report, this time concluding that Mick died of a blow to the left temple. Henri was charged with first degree murder and California filed extradition proceedings in Quebec.

Ashley stepped into my office the next day and said, "What do you think of this, Knute? Marcel Ney just called."

"Marcel, the coach of the Terreurs?"

"Right. He's coming over to talk to me. I assume it's about defending Henri."

I prayed that Marcel would decide to retain some other attorney. Ashley had again abandoned his diet and quit his training program. He was at least fifty pounds overweight. His skin was ashen, his eyes watery; by late afternoon his hands trembled from fatigue. He looked twenty years older than his fourty-four years. I feared that a major trial would destroy what little vitality he had left, but I also knew that Ashley was constitutionally unable to turn down a landmark case like *People v. Laval.*

Tired as he was from the strain of his kidnapping, his encounter with Angelo Manzoni, and his crushing trial schedule, Ashley agreed to undertake Henri's defense, but he warned Marcel, "It won't be an easy case, not if Emil Edison's videotape shows what the state claims it shows."

Marcel chuckled. "I've been checking on you, Mr Blackwood. Remember Ramona Krafft? Wasn't there a videotape of her little *crime passionel?*"

"Touché, Marcel! But Henri is not a charmer like our little Ramona."

That was the grossest understatement of Ashley's career. Henri had the gnarled frame of a stunted burr oak, the scarred face of an alley cat, and the bicuspids of a vampire. He walked with a crouch, as if speeding across the ice, and spoke with a snarl on his lips. Even at rest he seemed poised to inflict violence.

After our first interview with Henri, I asked Ashley if he had ever seen Henri smile.

"Only after he sticked Mick. But don't worry, Knute. For the trial we'll get him to look as jolly as Santa Claus."

"You mean happy pills?"

"All he can carry without falling."

Once it became public information that Ashley would defend Henri, the media clamored to learn who the prosecuting attorney would be. There was no answer to this question for over a week. I believe District Attorney Robespierre purposely delayed his decision to heighten public curiosity. On the day of the arraignment, he announced that Ginger Steinem would represent the people of California.

His choice was widely applauded by the California Bar. Since the *Gil Derais* trial, Ginger had won a number of victories in difficult cases, and her record of success persuaded many opposing attorneys to accept stringent plea bargains rather than take their chances at trial. She once said in a TV interview that her goal was to defeat Ashley in a capital case. Ginger had lost several pounds since the *Derais* case and attained a marathon level of fitness. The press, always obsessed by the outward appearance of women, termed her "the Aphrodite of the Bar."

"Well, well, Knute old chap," Ashley said when he heard of Ginger's appointment, "we're in for it now."

The prospect of once more crossing forensic swords with Ginger drove Ashley to expend the last limits of his energy in preparing our case. He embraced a strict diet and started daily work-out sessions with his fitness trainer. In thirty days, he lost eighteen pounds. Our public relations director, Fredrica Hill, inspected him every day to make certain that his shirts, ties, and suits were crisp and clean, and his shoes freshly shined.

Our first interview with Henri demonstrated his complete ignorance of the difficulties of his case. He ignored my lectures on the American legal system, the finest in the world in the way it protects the rights of the accused without unduly hampering the work of justice. He couldn't understand why we needed to call in a dozen experts to assist in his defense, why we had to spend weeks selecting the jury, or why we made motion after motion to suppress the evidence gathered by the police. He said a hundred times, "But, Monsieur, I have done no wrong. It was *un accidente*. I insist that you obtain my release *tres vite.*"

Henri's annoyance was heightened by the poor showing of the Terreurs following his incarceration. Deprived of his bloodlust, they lost most of their regular season games. It was clear they had no chance of advancing to the Stanley Cup without Henri at right wing.

"You *canailles* are costing me many dollars of bonus money," he said. "Go ask that cute Mademoiselle Steinem to let me out, and I promise on the head of my children that I will return to jail at the end of the season. In Trois Rivières my friends play their games and return to jail after *dîner.*"

I explained to him—to no avail—that, while work-release programs are indeed available for defendants charged with driving under the influence, they are not available to those held on capital charges.

Lacking a plan of defense, Ashley and I made *pro forma* motions to suppress the Edison videotapes and the pathology report, and lost on both issues. The press trumpeted that Ashley's winning touch had deserted him and that he was about to have his comeuppance at the hands of Ginger Steinem. On talk shows, law professors opined that Henri's case was unwinnable and that Ashley would bargain for a plea.

"That," said Ashley, "I would never do unless I thought we had no possibility of winning. It's a cop out."

The file was assigned to Judith Coke, an experienced judge who never tired under the pressure of a major case. When she summoned counsel to set a trial date, Ginger requested mid-July, and Ashley argued for late September. The judge put the case on the calendar for trial on Monday, August 17.

I asked Ashley why he had argued for the later date. He shook his head. "Knute, we can't be any worse off than we are now."

I don't know what Ashley thought might happen, but I respected his instincts. Maybe we would come across some new scrap of evidence, or a new witness would step forward, or there would be a ruling in another case which would provide us grounds to exclude the videotapes and the pathology reports.

Henri was furious that we had failed to clear him of all charges overnight. "Let's have the trial right now," he said. "Why wait until August? *Merde*! What is the problem? Get some hockey players on the jury. They understand how the game is played. You're taking your fucking time just to build up your fees." As he spoke, he brandished a newspaper editorial that called for a legislative commission to set a scale of fees for the legal profession.

To show Henri what we were up against and silence his complaints, I screened the Emil Edison videotape in his cell. Although full of jerks and shadows, it clearly revealed

Henri's hockey stick hitting Mick on the temple and Mick's immediate fall to the ice.

It is unfortunately true that our fees and expenses had nearly consumed Henri's assets. Although his years in professional hockey had brought him millions in salaries and royalties, he had spent his earnings on cars, houses, drink, and women. What little remained he had invested in the penny stocks of several Canadian mining companies, all now defunct. Ashley and I had to calculate every Friday evening which of Henri's assets we would auction to cover our charges for the past week. Although laymen deplore the amounts charged by criminal lawyers, the truth of the matter is that "big" cases seldom make money for the lawyers. They require staggering amounts of legal time, as well as the services of horrendously expensive expert witnesses. Lawyers end up taking home only a fraction of the total paid by the client.

When I returned to the office after another unpleasant interview with Henri, I told Ashley about Henri's desire to be released from jail during the day. "Our client has no idea what a difficult case we have. Frankly, I don't know how to deal with him. It's a real paradox. I don't want to discourage him, but then I don't want him to think that all we have to do is claim it was just an accident."

Instead of smiling, Ashley asked me to repeat what I'd just said.

"He wants us to say it was an accident."

"No, something before that."

I thought a moment and said, "I said how it was a paradox that—"

"Paradox, that's it." Ashley lapsed into one of his "trances" for several minutes. When his eyes opened, he said, "Yes, that's it! That's just it! Slow motion!"

I must have looked mystified, because Ashley smiled and said, "Don't you remember Zeno's paradoxes, Knute?"

"Sort of. Something like the arrow never hits the target because...."

"It keeps going half the remaining distance but never gets there."

"It went over my head."

"Never mind. Set up the Edison tape in the conference room and we'll look at it frame by frame."

I did as he suggested and we sat together watching the tape, first in slow motion, then one frame at a time. Emil's camcorder was old and battered, and its transport mechanism slipped and jerked, causing gaps in the picture. Gaps which were not apparent at normal speed were obvious in slow motion. The crucial sequence, the moment when Henri's stick moved up toward Mick's head and down again, lacked several frames. Nowhere did it show actual contact between Henri's hockey stick and Mick's head.

Ashley jumped up from the table. "There it is, Knute! You never actually see the blow land! You see the stick go up and down, and you assume it strikes Mick's head, but it never does."

"But how do you account for the fact that Mick drops dead?"

Ashley shook his head. "Knute, *I* don't account for it. That's the prosecutor's job. Our job is to show that there's no hard evidence that Henri caused Mick's death. We'll argue that his death could have resulted from some earlier injury, or that it was a condition which had been waiting to happen for years. Let Ginger try to deal with that!"

The trial began on August 17 as scheduled. Since our chances of victory depended on surprising the prosecution with our analysis of the Edison tape, we concealed our line of defense until the last possible moment. Ashley dismissed the prosecution witnesses, subject to the right to recall them during the defense's case. When the prosecution rested, I'm sure Ginger believed she was about to achieve her goal of a victory over Ashley. The media, having waited years for him to lose a major case, brayed, "Has Blackwood Been Trumped?" and "Has the Napoleon of the Courtroom Met His Waterloo?"

Ashley sprang the trap near the end of the first day of our case when he called back to the stand Dr Charles Bender, the state's forensic pathologist.

Q: [by Mr Blackwood] Dr Bender, you testified on direct examination, did you not, that the cause of decedent's death was a blow inflicted by the defendant to the left temple of Mr Milosevich?

A: [by Dr Bender] That was my testimony.

Q: You were not, however, present at the game between the Sachems and the Terreurs on April 10, 1992, were you?

A: No, sir, I was not.

Q: Therefore you did not have a chance to view the blow you claim was fatal, is that right?

A: That's correct.

Q: You testified, did you not, that the cause of death was a cerebrovascular event?

A: Yes, caused by a blow to the head.

Q: But, since you weren't an eyewitness, you don't know of your own knowledge whether or not the decedent sustained another blow to the head during the same game, do you?

A: Well, there was a clear sign of a blow to his head, and I assumed—

Q: You assumed. Dr Bender, when I ask you a question, I request that you not assume anything. Just tell me what you know for a fact. You testified, did you not, that Mr Milosevich's death was caused by a blow inflicted by the end of defendant's hockey stick, State's Exhibit 12?

A: Yes, I did.

Q: On what did you base that conclusion?

A: On my examination of Mr Edison's videotape and the coroner's report and my own inspection of the wound.

Q: On what basis did you conclude that the blow was caused by a hockey stick?

A: By its shape. The pattern of the injury conformed exactly to defendant's hockey stick.

Q: Why do you say defendant's hockey stick?

A: As I said, its shape.

Q: Isn't it a fact that there were many other hockey sticks in the Cow Palace at that game? Would it surprise you if I said that there were over 80?

A: Yes, that could be.

Q: Did you examine them all to see whether they had the same conformation as defendant's stick?

A: No.

Q: And why not?

A: Because defendant's was the only one weighted with lead.

Q: But you said you hadn't examined all the hockey sticks in the arena.

A: Well, no, because the tape—

Q: The Edison tape?

A: Yes. It clearly showed the landing of defendant's stick on Mick's head.

Q: Very well. I will ask you to watch the Edison tape with me and tell me where you see the blow on which you base your opinion. Mr Rockne, will you please screen for us State's Exhibit 6?

[Judge Coke ordered the court room darkened. State's Exhibit 6 played until frame 1312]

Q: [by Mr Blackwood] Now, Dr Bender, Mr Rockne will advance the picture frame by frame. I will ask you to tell me where you see a blow land on Mr Milosevich's temple. Will you do that?

A: Yes, sir.

Q: Is it here?

A: No.

Q: Is it here?

A: No.

[Multiple repetitions of the same question and answer omitted. On the conclusion of the screening:]

Q: [by Mr Blackwood] Am I correct, Dr Bender, in saying that you didn't at any point see defendant's stick actually touch Mr Milosevich's left temple?

A: When you play it at normal speed, it is very evident, but when you slow it down—

Q: Dr Bender, please. I remind you that we played the tape frame by frame, and you said you didn't see the stick touch the decedent.

A: Sure, at slow speed, but—

Q: At normal speed, you're going to say, you saw the blow?

A: That's right.

Q: Isn't it more truthful to say that your eyes imagined the blow?

A: You can't fool the eyes.

Q: Are you familiar with the 1989 Motional Vision Study of Dr E.M. Mallard?

A: I've read it.

Q: And what does it conclude that relates to this case? [by Ms Steinem] Objection, your Honor.

[by Mr Blackwood] On what grounds, counsel?

[by the Court] Yes, what are your grounds?

[by Ms Steinem] Relevance, Your Honor.

[by Mr Blackwood] It seems to me, Your Honor, that the witness testified that you can't fool the eyes. We believe our examination of the tape with this witness shows that his eyes were indeed fooled.

[by the Court] Overruled. The witness will answer.

[by Dr Bender] A: Dr Mallard's study concluded that the

eye can, under certain circumstances, derive a pattern not actually presented by the object under scrutiny.

Q: Can you elaborate on how his conclusions are relevant to this case, or shall I?

A: The eye completes motions in accordance with patterns lodged in the brain through prior experience.

Q: The study says specifically, does it not, that when the eyes perceive one object moving toward a second object, and then perceives the first object moving away from the second object, the brain assumes that the second object was the target of the first object? Is that a fair summary?

A: That's about what it said.

Q: So, to apply Dr Mallard's conclusion to this case, when your eyes saw the hockey stick going towards Mick's head and then saw it going back down again, the brain stepped in and assumed that the stick hit Mick's head. Is that correct?

A: Yes, that's what he argued.

Q: And is Dr Mallard respected for his research in the field of perception?

A: Yes.

Q: Now, let's get back to a question I asked you earlier. You testified that the cause of Mr Milosevich's death was an aneurysm, did you not?

A: Yes, sir.

Q: Now, isn't it true that aneurysms often occur spontaneously and may be also referred to as cerebrovascular accidents?

A: Yes.

Q: And cerebrovascular accidents are the most frequent cause of death, right after heart attacks and cancer?

A: Yes.

Q: What is the popular name for a cerebrovascular accident?

A: A stroke.

Q: And many people, old and young, die of strokes every year?

A: Yes.

Q: In most cases, Doctor, is a stroke caused by a blow or, in your language, a trauma?

A: No, usually it is spontaneous.

Q: An artery in the brain bursts of its own accord?

A: Right.

Q: And sometimes the patient dies, and sometimes he or she is paralyzed to a greater or lesser degree, and sometimes he or she recovers completely?

A: Yes, results vary.

Q: Let me ask you, Doctor, could Mr Milosevich have died as a result of a spontaneous stroke, a stroke resulting from some inherited weakness in his system, rather than a blow?

A: I suppose it is possible, but—

Q: Or could he could have died from some weakness resulting from a blow years before, or a blow delivered in the same game by someone other than the defendant?

A: Possibly.

Q: Very possible. It's quite common in your experience, is it not, that people die of strokes, or cerebrovascular accidents as you call them, not directly related to any recent trauma?

A: Yes.

Q: No further questions.

Ginger Steinem had not anticipated this bombshell. She had let her case depend on one expert's analysis of the Edison tape. All she could do at this point late in the afternoon was to have Dr Bender repeat what he had said on direct examination and hope that the judge would adjourn the trial for the day. Ashley forestalled her by rising to object that Dr Bender's testimony was repetitious. Judge Coke sustained his objections.

Having found myself in a few difficult situations in my career, I sympathized with Ginger's frustration. She faced the eye of a national television audience and had several times declared that the state couldn't fail to obtain a verdict of guilty. Such is the fallacy of building a case where each step rests on the foundation of the preceding step. As I stated in my description of the *Strafford* case, it is not enough to show the motive—Mick's supposed seduction of Henri's Juliette—or the means—Henri's weighted stick. The prosecution must also prove that means and motive united in the commission of a crime. For this, Ginger relied on the Edison tape. When its probative value was demolished, she had no other proof to fall back on.

She pleaded for a week's delay, saying that it was just a matter of time to find other films that would give a clearer picture of the encounter, or an eyewitness who had been close enough to see in detail the fatal blow.

The court allowed her until noon the next day, but no more. In fact, a month would not have given her time enough to locate the evidence she needed. Death had occurred in a split-second during a flurry of punches and counter punches. The view from the back was blocked by the boards and the view from across the ice was obscured by Henri's head. If an eyewitness claimed to have seen the blow, we expected to show that his "memory" derived from the endless television screenings of the Edison tape and the conclusions of its medical commentators.

The next morning the state's case lay drying on the beach. Both sides rested.

As Ashley stood to give his closing argument, he made eye contact with each juror, one at a time, then began speaking in a tone of calm reason, like a law professor. As he progressed, his voice rose in intensity until, when he reached his summation, passion inflamed each word.

"Ladies and gentlemen, let us take a look at the state's case. Their evidence is a bunch of 'maybes.' 'Maybe' Henri had a grudge against Mick. 'Maybe' he hit him with his hockey stick. 'Maybe' the blow contributed to Mick's death.

"'Maybe, maybe, maybe.' You don't have to be a lawyer to argue just as well the other way. 'Maybe' Henri knew the stories about Mick and Josephine were concocted by the press. 'Maybe' Mick's death resulted from a trauma years ago. Or 'maybe' it resulted from a genetic defect, an accident of nature.

"Judge Coke will instruct you that the state cannot build a case on a bunch of 'maybe this's' and 'maybe that's.' The test is not whether you think defendant might have killed Mr Milosevich, but whether you are sure of it 'beyond a reasonable doubt.' If you say 'maybe' Henri inflicted a fatal injury on Mick, you can just as well say 'maybe' some other player inflicted it in this game or some other game.

"If 'maybes' convict, any of us in this courtroom could be guilty of Mick's death, but 'maybes' don't have that power. So I am confident that you will return a verdict that tells the state it cannot convict a man or woman on the basis of some 'maybes.'"

Ginger made a long and eloquent plea to convict, this time basing her case more on motive and inference, and less on the Edison tape. Judge Coke read her instructions to the jury. They retired and returned the next day with a unanimous verdict of acquittal.

I looked at Ginger right after the foreperson spoke the words "not guilty." It is hard to say whether her face reflected anger or grief. Until the last day of testimony she had been certain she would achieve her goal of defeating Ashley in a capital case. She must have believed he would try to confuse the jury with statements that hockey is a "rough game," that "accidents happen," and so forth. No doubt she had prepared excellent rebuttals to arguments he never made. Like many a commander, she was fighting the wrong war.

As the foreperson read the verdict, I watched the expression on Ashley's face and wondered whether the affection he had felt for Ginger at the time of the *Gil Derais* case lingered with him, or whether he felt avenged for her lack of response to his previous overtures. Would he wait for her to cross the courtroom and congratulate him on his victory, or would he walk to her and make some comforting remarks?

The next instant all thoughts of Ginger Steinem fled my mind. The courtroom erupted in a babel of shouts in French, English, and Russian. Henri hugged and kissed Ashley repeatedly on both cheeks and headed for me, his fangs bared by his smile. I took refuge behind a bailiff. A group of Henri's teammates led by coach Marcel Ney carried Ashley out of the courthouse on their shoulders to a night of merriment which resulted in the accidental destruction of a bar in the North Beach area.

Newspaper headlines the next morning blazed messages very different from those of the previous days. A sampling:

ASHLEY TORPEDOES S.S. STEINEM

BLACKWOOD BEATS THE BABE; IS HE INVINCIBLE?

I wondered how long the praise—if it was praise—would last. When I saw Ashley late the next day, I asked him what Rule he had for the *Laval* case.

"That's a tough one. I'd say: *WHEN IT'S HOPELESS, ATTACK THEIR STRONGEST POINT.*"

Brutus and Alexander pressured me to write Henri and ask for his autograph. He sent two autographed hockey sticks and a letter saying he hoped they would excel in hockey as their father excelled in the law. The letter hangs in a gold frame over my desk.

TEN

The *Laval* case raised Ashley once more to celebrity status. Each day brought a mail sack full of requests for interviews and speeches accompanied by generous honoraria. When he stepped outside the office, cameras blazed like chain lightning. His face appeared in the media twice for President Bush's once.

As surely as the Nile engenders toads, Ashley's victory triggered a hyperperistaltic flow of invective from the bowels of the press and the organized Bar. They memorialized him as "a vulture feeding on the corpse of justice," "the champion swimmer in the cesspools of the law," and "a lawyer who feasts on the roadkill of crime."

The obloquy of the media wafted far above the heads of the nation's sports-lovers. Ashley received lifetime passes to all professional hockey games. Marcel Ney designated him as the "Courtroom Coach" of the Terreurs, fitted him with a team uniform, and saved him a place on their bench. When the Terreurs won the Stanley Cup in 1993, Henri presented Ashley a gold hockey stick engraved with the names of the players and coaches.

More cases were offered to Blackwood & Associates than we could service, even after we increased our staff to the point where lawyers had to share offices. To meet the demands on his time, Ashley and I worked out an arrangement where First and Second-Degree Associates prepared the cases, one or more Third-Degree Associates conducted the trials under my supervision, and Ashley made the closing arguments. The efficient deployment of our resources allowed Ashley to appear in two or three cases a week. He never failed to amaze me by his ability to read hundreds of pages of testimony overnight and assemble from the questions and answers a persuasive closing statement. Some critics seized on the fact that Blackwood & Associates lost a greater percentage of its cases in 1993 than in the previous five years. They neglected to note, however, that most of our new cases were ones that other attorneys had abandoned as hopeless. Within a year, the firm doubled its net income and Ashley commissioned his architect, Michaelangelo Brunelli, to draw plans for an addition to our office facilities. But the stress of our new system undermined Ashley's constitution. His review of the transcripts, his court appearances, and his nightly conferences with the trial lawyers, left him barely three hours of sleep a day. He overate to combat persistent fatigue and regained the eighteen pounds he had lost before the *Laval* case.

I stopped him one morning as he prepared to leave for court and pleaded with him to take a long vacation.

"It's all right, Knute," he said. "Let's keep going a few more years, then we'll retire."

"You won't last two more months the way you're going."

He patted me on the back. "You're a worrywart, old pal. I'm fine and we're doing great."

"Ashley, I beg you. Take a month, go to Asia, lie on a beach, visit a temple. By the time you're back, the office addition will be finished."

"Why now? In a year or two we'll be basking on the sands of the Riviera."

"Sure," I said, shifting to a lighter tone, "but I want to arrive there with a snorkel mask, not an oxygen tank. And I'd like my eyes to be good enough to tell a man from a woman."

"You, Knute? Mamie will keep you in reading glasses so you won't be able to see anyone more than an arm's length from your nose."

Ashley agreed to a short break from work to visit his parents in August, 1994. Herb and Adele had completed an addition to their cabin at Lake Kakabeetowatachee and wanted him to join them in the lakes and forests of northern Minnesota. Most Minnesotans look forward to a week in the cool air of the North Woods, far from the hives of humanity, but Ashley was a city boy who viewed the outdoors as the breeding place of a thousand venomous insects. Being a good son, though, he gave in to his mother's pleas and flew to Lake Kakabeetowatachee.

The day after he arrived, he called me from Tenstrike, the nearest town, to say that he was having a miserable time. "The food is all potato chips and walleye pike. There isn't a damn thing to do except swat mosquitoes and listen to my father bitch about taxes and welfare."

On his return he brought me some news I found extremely disturbing. Every time he left the cabin, he said, someone in a rusty Ford sedan followed him. He couldn't draw close enough to read the license plate or get a good look at the driver, but he had the impression it was a young man. Herb had also noticed that they were being followed. He had sensed their pursuer before Ashley had and never went outside without tucking a pistol in his belt. He cast himself as Ashley's personal bodyguard and hung at his elbow day and night, to the point of sleeping on a cot at the foot of his bed. For five days Ashley had no respite from his father's monologues.

Ashley pretended that the incident was of no consequence, but admitted it had stirred up memories of his kidnapping. I asked him to think of anyone who might hold a grudge against him since the death of Amy and Edmund Mortimer. He said he had sifted his brain and couldn't come up with an answer. "I thought of all the prosecutors who had lost 'open and shut cases' to me," he said, "and all the cops who have it in for me. But why would they go to Minnesota when they could put me away in a nice, tidy drive-by shooting in San Francisco?"

"Do you think he was following Herb and not you?"

"No. Dad said he was never followed except when I was with him."

I tried to persuade Ashley to hire a bodyguard. He said it would be a waste of time. "It would just get two guys killed instead of one." A further example of his selfless concern for others.

On my own motion, I took two precautions. First, I

bought a policy on Ashley's life much larger than the one I had bought after the shooting on the courthouse steps in 1984. Next, I asked Sergeant Kesselring to retain a Minnesota investigator to find out who had been following Ashley around Lake Kakabeetowatachee.

To be honest, my fears far exceeded Ashley's. When I walked with him from the courthouse in the evening fogs, I imagined a rusty Ford lurking in the shadows, footsteps behind us, the echo of a gunshot in the night, and a ski-masked figure, briefly illumined by the yellow glow of a street light, running away into the darkness.

I tried to repress my anxiety by immersing myself in the defense of Wolfgang Kreuziger, the Satanist who sacrificed small children to Moloch, and Peter Vesalius, a Renaissance historian who dismembered prostitutes. Yet every day I felt an aura of danger about me, the same way Mamie "smells trouble coming."

Gloomy forebodings were far from my mind on October 17, 1994, the day before Ashley was to start on the vacation planned in secrecy by me and his secretary, Maxine Gregg: a month-long trip around the world! It was far overdue. Ashley looked awful. He was flushed and tired to the point of slurring his words. The evening before his departure, I pleaded with him to have a good night's sleep before his long flight to the Orient. But he insisted on attending an exhibition game pitting the Trois Rivières Terreurs against their old enemies, the Saskatchewan Sachems.

The clash of the Terreurs and the Sachems must have

satisfied the bloodlust of the most savage hockey fan. Hardly a minute passed without two or three men in the penalty box. Opposing players never missed an opportunity to inflict a punishing body check, and full-scale brawls erupted at five-minute intervals.

Ashley sat on the players' bench right in front of me. His thoughts were still on his work, and I had to prod him to cheer and boo along with the team.

Towards the end of the second period, when the cacophony of the crowd was at its height, a young, blond man brushed in front of me, temporarily blocking my view of the play. I heard a loud noise as he passed. Because of the roars of the audience and the shouts of the Terreurs in front of me, I dismissed it as just another noisemaker until I saw Ashley slumped over, his head between his knees, blood pooling around his shoes.

I reacted at once. I rose and pointed to the murderer. "Stop that man!" I yelled at the top of my lungs. "Ashley's been shot!"

The murderer struggled to break through the crowd, but the aisles were clogged with people streaming out for intermission refreshments. At my second shout two brawny fans and a security guard stopped him. A dozen Terreurs leaped from the bench, skates and all, and punched their way through the crowd to the murderer. Some held him, others pummeled him and a few bystanders to boot. Only my presence persuaded them to limit themselves to forcible restraint. When the uniformed police appeared and took charge of the assassin, I shouldered my way back to the players' bench to see Ashley.

Henri Laval and Marcel Ney had lifted him onto a stretcher. Tears streamed from their eyes. I steeled myself to look. Part of his face had been blown away by the blast. One bullet had ended the life of the nation's greatest lawyer. I took his hand and whispered, "Goodbye, Ashley." It was all I could manage through my tears.

The police dragged the murderer past me and exited through a locker room. The lad's face looked as if it had been worked over with a baseball bat; blood streamed from his forehead, his scalp, and his nostrils.

That evening I learned from my friend Sergeant Kesselring that Ashley's murderer was one Roger Mortimer, the twenty-six-year-old son of Edmund and Amy Mortimer. In his confession he said his sole purpose in life was to avenge the death of his parents, for which he held Ashley responsible. Roger insisted that his mother had appeared to him in a dream the day after her death and revealed that Ashley had bribed agent Javert to stage her and Edmund's murder as a failed kidnapping. He denied that his parents had any intention of kidnapping Ashley; all they wanted was for Ashley to provide funds for Roger's new house.

Otto Krabick, the lawyer Marty Vickers (alias "Machine-Gun Marty") had rejected as counsel because of his foul language, was assigned to defend Roger. He argued that Roger, believing that Ashley had marked him next in line for execution after his parents, acted in self-defense. Krabick's theory caused a flutter in the tabloid press, but was laughed out of the jury room. Roger was convicted of first-degree murder and sentenced to twenty years in prison. I couldn't help but wonder how Ashley would have defended the boy. Would he at last have entered a plea of insanity?

Though Ashley earned his fame in California, Herb and Adele insisted that the funeral take place in Minneapolis. They bought three plots in Dreamland Park so that they could rest with him until called to the Final Judgment. They tried to keep the funeral a secret from all but me, Alexia, and a few close friends, but someone leaked the time and place of the service, and many of the men and women Ashley had defended attended his last appearance.

I asked Henry Laval and his teammates to form an honor guard to keep the media away, a job they performed with such enthusiasm that I had to bail out a dozen of them that evening. Matt Tyler appeared, not in a battered Fiat, but a new Jaguar he had bought from his share of the proceeds of *The Lonely Assassin*, the movie made about his murder of Congressman Waller.

Marty Vickers had completed his sentence for manslaughter with years off for good behavior. He flew to Minneapolis and insisted on reading an eulogy he had composed in Ashley's honor. It lasted nearly an hour and forced me to omit the eulogy I had been working on for the past week.

Ramona promised to be at the service, but I never saw her until the graveside ceremony when she waved to me from the back of a converted van.

I hoped that Ellen Strafford would come. Instead, she sent me a scented note regretting that business affairs kept her in the Mideast and saying she would forever thank Allah for Ashley's and my help. Yet I wondered whether she might be the mysterious veiled woman who stood at the back of the chapel beside a man in sunglasses who bore a marked resemblance to Nikos Callimachus.

After his kidnapping, Ashley had repeatedly promised me to disclose his financial situation. When I pressed him for information about his will and estate, he put me off with vague assurances that we would talk about it soon. Like many who deal with death on a daily basis, he avoided thoughts of his own mortality.

I searched everywhere for his will, but found none. Then I spent months trying to discover the true state of his financial affairs. He had put aside some ten million dollars for his retirement, but, unfortunately, had entrusted his savings to John Law, a financial planner for many Hollywood celebrities. The results had been disastrous for every one but John Law. I stood amazed at the variety of the investments he had selected for Ashley: films which never reached the public, hedge funds which bet the wrong way on the market, real estate developments stymied by interminable environmental impact statements, and coal properties idled by falling oil prices. Not one listed stock, not one government bond, not even a money market fund!

Ashley, no doubt, had been too immersed in client concerns to pay attention to his investments. I avoided his mistakes by delegating the management of my assets to Mamie and was delighted with the twenty percent returns she averaged year after year.

Not long after Ashley's interment, there arose the kinds

of disputes which inevitably follow great men past their graves. I was disappointed when Alexia, whom I had never suspected of any mercenary motivation, filed a claim against the assets of Ashley's estate on the grounds that she was his common-law wife and entitled to one-half of his community property. Since they had never lived together, her claim was summarily dismissed. Then a lawyer for Stanford University walked into my office waving Ashley's pledge of one million dollars in my face. It was the same pledge that had been publicized in 1991, much to Ashley's embarrassment and annoyance. Stanford claimed that the estate owed it a balance of $990,000. Unfortunately, the estate was strapped to pay its court fees, or I would gladly have complied.

Stanford played a role in another part of Ashley's history, which, as his impartial biographer, I feel obligated to disclose. During my research on Ashley's life, I analyzed his high school records. I was impressed, but not surprised, that, despite all the time he spent on A&A Social Services, he managed to attain top grades in his classwork, as well as citations for his extra-curricular activities.

My discussions with the school staff, however, led me to the shocking conclusion that Ashley had falsified his transcript in order to obtain admission to Stanford University! Apparently an assistant principal who suffered from pressing financial needs had changed Ashley's grades from Cs or Ds to As or A pluses. He had also inserted in the transcript a sheaf of reports allegedly penned by teachers, coaches, and school counselors, all praising Ashley's accomplishments in track, debate, student government, and community outreach.

In all candor, I must confess that these forgeries were highly inappropriate. Still, taking the long view, it must be conceded that Ashley had to act as he did in order to fulfill his destiny as the nation's greatest criminal lawyer. Admission to Stanford was an essential part of his career plan; he had no alternative but to take the steps necessary to this end. Who now could wish that this champion of justice had followed any other path? No one was injured, no one lost money as a result of his deception, and he alleviated the financial problems of an under-compensated assistant principal.

Whatever the argument about the means, Ashley attained his ends. He received early acceptance at Stanford and within a few years the country was treated to the spectacle of nearly a hundred trials, each one demonstrating a genius in jurisprudence not likely to be surpassed by future generations.

Blackwood & Associates did not long survive Ashley. I proposed that the Third-Degree Associates form a partnership with myself as the Managing Partner. My proposal was talked to death, as frequently occurs with lawyers. The firm dissolved and each attorney went his own way. The bank foreclosed on the Blackwood Building; Mike Brunelli's Georgian masterpiece was demolished to make room for a sterile residential development.

With Mamie's hearty agreement, I decided that fourteen years in the law were enough. Between our accumulated savings and the proceeds from my two insurance policies on Ashley, we possessed the means to buy a cabin in the Boundary Waters to use as a base for visits to our families and childhood friends.

A few years before Ashley's death, I had started compiling notes about his life and trials, thinking I might someday make them into a book. Viewing the success of other lawyers in selling their courtroom memoirs, I decided, with the encouragement of Mamie and a few friends, to study writing and share my insights with the public. "It's better than playing golf all day," Mamie pointed out, "and a lot less expensive."

It was only natural to dedicate my first published work to the man who was my friend, colleague, and mentor.

Such was the life of Ashley Blackwood, the greatest legal mind seen by the criminal Bar in this century. The list of his most famous cases—Matt Tyler, Ellen Strafford, Ramona Krafft, Reginald Lothbrook, Marty Vickers, Gil Derais, and Henri Laval, to name a few—would entitle a lawyer with three times his years to a secure niche in the Pantheon of United States jurisprudence, perhaps even an appointment to the United States Supreme Court.

I leave my readers to form their own opinions about Ashley's contributions to the cause of justice. I am sure that, when they look at the whole record, they will join with me in viewing him as the single greatest trial advocate in our nation's history.

I commissioned Michaelangelo Brunelli to design at my expense a monument for his grave in Dreamland Park. On it I summarized his life as follows:

IN MEMORIAM

ASHLEY BLACKWOOD
THE ULTIMATE
CRIMINAL LAWYER